PENGUIN

The Little Man from Archangel

Georg̱̱̱ C̱ristian Simenon w̱ ̱ on 12 February 1903 in Li ̱ge, Belgium. He ̱ egan work as a repoṟ̱ ̱ a local news-pap̱ ̱ t the age of sixteen, and at nineteen he mov̱ ̱to Paris to emba̱k on a career as a novelist. He started by writing ̱ p-fiction nov ̱s and novellas published, under various pseudony̱ms, from 192̱ onwards. He went on to write seventy-five Maigret novels aṉ wenty-eight Maigret short stories.

̱ though Simenon is best known in Britain as the writer of the Ma̱ret books, his prolific output of over 400 novels made him a ho̱̱ehold name and institution in Continental Europe, where mṵ h of his work is constantly in print. The dark realism of Si̱enon's books has lent them naturally to screen adaptation.

S̱menon died in 1989 in Lausanne, Switzerland, where he had live̱ for the latter part of his life.

GEORGES SIMENON

The Little Man from Archangel

Translated by Nigel Ryan

PENGUIN BOOKS

PENGUIN BOOKS

Published by the Penguin Group
Penguin Books Ltd, 80 Strand, London WC2R ORL, England
Penguin Group (USA) Inc., 375 Hudson Street, New York, New York 10014, USA
Penguin Books Australia Ltd, 250 Camberwell Road, Camberwell, Victoria 3124, Australia
Penguin Books Canada Ltd, 10 Alcorn Avenue, Toronto, Ontario, Canada M4V 3B2
Penguin Books India (P) Ltd, 11, Community Centre, Panchsheel Park, New Delhi – 110 017, India
Penguin Group (NZ), Cnr Airborne and Rosedale Roads, Albany, Auckland 1310, New Zealand
Penguin Books (South Africa) (Pty) Ltd, 24 Sturdee Avenue, Rosebank 2196, South Africa

Penguin Books Ltd, Registered Offices: 80 Strand, London WC2R ORL, England

www.penguin.com

Le Petit homme d'Arkhangelsk first published 1956
This translation first published by Hamish Hamilton 1957
Published in Penguin Books 1964
Reissued with minor revisions in Penguin Classics 2004
1

Set in 9.75/13.25 pt Trump Mediaeval
Typeset by Rowland Phototypesetting Ltd, Bury St Edmunds, Suffolk
Printed in England by Clays Ltd, St Ives plc

Chapter One

He made the mistake of telling a lie. He felt it intuitively the moment he opened his mouth to reply to Fernand Le Bouc, and it was actually from timidity, lack of sangfroid, that he did not alter the words which came to his lips.

What he said was:

'She's gone to Bourges.'

Le Bouc asked, as he rinsed a glass behind his counter:

'Is La Loute still there?'

He replied without looking at him:

'I suppose so.'

It was ten o'clock in the morning, and as it was Thursday the market was in full swing. In Fernand's small bistro, almost entirely enclosed in glass, on the corner of the Impasse des Trois-Rois, five or six men were standing at the bar. At that moment it didn't matter who was there, but this was to become important, and Jonas Milk was later to try to identify each face.

Near him was Gaston Ancel, the red-faced butcher, in his blood-stained apron, who came in three or four times a morning for a quick glass of white wine and who had a particular way of wiping his mouth afterwards. He was constantly cracking jokes in his loud voice and, in his butcher's shop, used to tease the customers, while at the cash desk Madame Ancel apologized for her husband's bad language.

With Ancel, a cup of coffee in his hand, stood Benaiche, the policeman on duty at the market, known to everybody as Julien.

The little old man with the greenish coat and trembling hands must have spent the night outside, as he did most of the time. Nobody knew who he was, nor where he came from, but they had got used to him and he had ended up by becoming part of the surroundings.

Who were the others? An electrician whom Jonas didn't know, with someone whose pocket was stuffed with pencils, a foreman or the boss of some small business.

He never recalled the sixth, but he could have sworn that there was a figure between himself and the window.

At the tables behind the men, three or four women vegetable vendors dressed in black were eating sandwiches.

It was the same atmosphere as on any market morning, that is to say, on Tuesdays, Thursdays, and Saturdays. That Thursday a clear and warm June sun beat down full on the fronts of the houses, while under the huge roof of the covered-in market the people were bustling round the hampers and stalls in a bluish half-light.

Jonas had been anxious to avoid any hitch in his routine. As ten o'clock approached, his shop being free of customers, he had walked the five yards of pavement which separated him from Fernand's bistro, and from there, through the windows, he could watch the boxes of second-hand books arrayed against his shop front.

He could quite well not have opened his mouth. Some of them, at Fernand's, used to go up to the bar without a word, for it was known in advance what they were going to have. For him, it was invariably an espresso coffee.

Even so he said, possibly out of humility, or from a need to be precise: 'An espresso coffee.'

Practically everyone knew everyone else, and sometimes they didn't say good morning to each other, thinking they had already met earlier in the day.

Fernand Le Bouc, for example, was on his feet from three o'clock in the morning for the arrival of the lorries, and Ancel, the butcher, who awoke at five, had already been in at least twice to the bar.

The shops were clustered round the slate roof of the market, which had no walls and was bordered by a gutter littered with broken crates and packing-cases, rotting oranges, and trampled wood shavings.

The housewives who trod in this debris had no idea that the square, before their arrival, long before they were awake, had already seen, amidst the noise of heavy lorries and the smell of diesel oil, several hours of feverish existence.

Jonas was watching the coffee falling drop by drop from the tiny chromium tap into the brown cup. He had another habit: before being handed his coffee he would unwrap the transparent paper containing his two pieces of sugar.

'Is Gina all right?' Le Bouc had asked him.

He had at first replied:

'She's all right.'

It was only because of what Fernand said next that he felt obliged to tell a lie.

'I was wondering if she was ill. I haven't seen her this morning.'

The butcher interrupted his conversation with the policeman to remark:

'That's funny! I haven't seen her either.'

Normally Gina did her shopping early, in bedroom slippers, often without combing her hair, sometimes in a sort of flowered dressing-gown affair, before the arrival of the crowds.

Jonas opened his mouth, and it was then that, despite his instinct which told him it was unwise, he could not bring himself to change the words he had prepared:

'She's gone to Bourges.'

From time to time his wife did happen to go to Bourges to

3

see La Loute, as she was called, the daughter of the grain merchant over the way, who had been living there for the past two years. But almost invariably, as everyone must have known, she took the half past eleven bus.

He was annoyed by his reply, not only because it was a lie and he did not like telling lies, but because something told him it was a mistake. Yet he couldn't reveal the truth, still less so because at any moment Palestri, Gina's father, would be climbing out of his carrier-tricycle to come and have a drink.

It was the butcher who asked, addressing no one in particular:

'Does anybody really know what La Loute does in Bourges?'

And Fernand, indifferently:

'Whoring, probably.'

It was strange that the butcher should have been present just then and taken part in the conversation, because his own daughter Clémence, the eldest, the one who was married, had been more or less mixed up in the affair.

Jonas was drinking his piping hot coffee in little sips, and the steam was misting over his glasses, which made him look different from the way he usually looked.

'See you later,' he said, placing the money on the linoleum of the counter.

Nobody had touched the books in the two boxes. It was rare for him to sell any during the market, and in the morning he hardly ever did more than a few exchanges. Mechanically he straightened the books, glanced at the window display and went into his shop where there was a sweet smell of dust and mildewed paper.

He hadn't dared to visit Clémence, the butcher's daughter, that night, but he had seen her a short time before, doing her shopping while she pushed the baby in its pram. He had gone up to her, deliberately.

'Good morning, Clémence.'

'Good morning, Monsieur Jonas.'

If she called him 'Monsieur', it was because she was twenty-two years old while he was forty. She had been at school with Gina. Both of them were born in the Place du Vieux-Marché. Gina was the daughter of Palestri, the greengrocer who, while his wife kept shop, delivered the orders in his three-wheeler.

'Nice day!' he had called out again, peering at Clémence through his thick lenses.

'Yes. It looks as if it's going to be a hot one.'

He bent over to look at the baby, Poupou, who was enormous.

'He's growing!' he observed gravely.

'I think he's cutting his first tooth. Give my love to Gina!'

All this was at about nine o'clock. As she uttered her last remark, Clémence had glanced into the back of the shop as if she were expecting to catch sight of her friend in the kitchen.

She hadn't seemed embarrassed. Pushing Poupou's pram before her, she had moved off towards Chaigne's, the grocer's, and gone into the shop.

That meant that Gina had lied, and Jonas had been almost sure of it since the evening before. He had shut the shop as usual at seven o'clock, or rather he had closed the door without removing the handle, for as long as he stayed up there was no point in missing a customer, and some of them used to come fairly late, to exchange their books from the lending library department. From the kitchen it was possible to hear the bell which the door operated when it opened. The house was narrow, one of the oldest in the Place du Vieux-Marché, with a coat-of-arms still carved on one of the stones and the date 1596.

'Dinner's ready!' Gina had called out, while at the same time he could hear a sizzling sound from the oven.

'I'm coming.'

She was wearing a tight-fitting red cotton dress. He had never dared to say a word to her on that subject. She had large breasts and ample haunches and she always made her dressmaker give her close-fitting dresses, beneath which she wore only a slip and a brassière, so that when she moved even the contour of her navel was outlined.

It was fish that she was cooking, and before it there was sorrel soup. They did not lay a tablecloth, but ate on the oil-cloth, and often Gina did not take the trouble to use dishes, merely putting the pans straight on the table.

Outside, with strangers, she was gay, with a naughty sparkle in her eye, a smile at her lips, and she laughed all the more for having dazzling white teeth.

She was the most beautiful girl in the market, everyone was agreed, even if some of them made certain reservations or put on a disapproving expression when she came into the conversation. Alone with Jonas her face would darken. Sometimes the transformation was noticeable the moment she crossed the doorway of the shop. Gaily she would throw out some last jest to a passer-by, and in the time it took her to turn round to enter the house, her face would lose all expression, her walk was no longer the same, and if she still swayed her hips it was with a sudden lassitude.

They sometimes ate without uttering a word, as quickly as possible, as if to have done with a chore, and he would still be at table when she began, behind his back, to wash up the dishes at the sink.

Had they spoken that evening? As he hadn't known then what was afoot, he had not noticed, but he could not recall a single remark being said.

The old market-place, so teeming with life in the morning, was becoming very calm as the evening drew on, and there was only the sound of the cars passing in the rue de Bourges, more than a hundred yards away, a mother calling from time to time from her doorway to her children who had lingered on under the great slate roof.

While she was washing up she had announced:

'I'm going to see Clémence.'

The butcher's eldest daughter had married an employee at the waterworks two years before and it had been a fine wedding at which everyone from the square had been present. She was called Reverdi now and the young family lived in a flat in the rue des Deux-Ponts.

As he did not press his wife for an explanation she had added, turning her back to him:

'There's a film they want to see.'

On those occasions Gina would sometimes go and sit with the baby, which was only eight months old. She would take a book with her, and the key, and would not be back until midnight, for the Reverdis went to the second house.

The lights hadn't been turned on yet. There was enough daylight from the window and the door into the backyard. The air was bluish, of an extraordinary stillness, as it often is at the end of very long summer days. Some birds were twittering in the lime tree belonging to Chaigne the grocer, the only tree in the whole cluster of houses, in the middle of an enormous yard cluttered with barrels and crates.

Gina had gone upstairs. The staircase rose not from the kitchen, but from the little room separating it from the shop, which Jonas called his office.

When she came down again, she had neither hat nor coat on. Actually she only wore a hat for going to Mass on Sundays. On other days she went about bareheaded, her brown hair all untidy and, when it fell on her cheek, she would flick it back with a toss of her head.

'See you later!'

He had noticed that she was clutching close to her the large rectangular patent-leather bag which he had given her for her last birthday. He had almost called her back to say:

'You're forgetting your book.'

But she was already away down the pavement, walking

briskly, almost running in the direction of the rue des Pré-montrés. He had remained a little while on the doorstep, following her with his eyes, then just breathing in the still warm air of the evening and watching the lamps which were beginning to light up, to the left, in the rue de Bourges.

What had he done until midnight? The boxes of books which he used to put on the pavement in the morning had been brought in. He had changed the places of a few volumes for no particular reason except to arrange them by the colour of their covers. He had switched on the light. There were books everywhere, on the shelves up to the ceiling and in piles on the counter, on the floor in the corners. They were second-hand books, nearly all of them worn, dirty, held together with sticking-paper, and he lent out more of them than he sold.

On one side of the room could be seen only old bindings, seventeenth- and eighteenth-century editions, an old La Fontaine published in Belgium, a Latin bible with curious engravings, some Bourdaloue sermons, five copies in different formats of *Télémaque*, then below, more recent collections such as *The History of the Consulate and the Empire* bound in dark green.

Jonas didn't smoke. Apart from coffee, he did not drink either. He only went to the cinema once in a while to please Gina. Did it really please Gina? He wasn't sure. She insisted on it, however, as she insisted on taking a *loge*, which to her way of thinking showed that she was a married woman.

He didn't hold it against her. He didn't hold anything against her, even now. By what right could he have expected anything from her?

His little office-room, between the shop and the kitchen, had no window, received no air except through the two doors, and here, too, there were books up to the ceiling. But most important of all, in the desk at which he never sat down without a sigh of satisfaction, were his books on philately and his stamps.

For he wasn't just a second-hand bookseller. He was a stamp dealer. And if his shop, squeezed between the food shops of the Vieux-Marché, was not much to look at, the local shopkeepers would have been surprised to learn that the name of Jonas Milk was known by dealers and collectors the world over.

In a drawer within arm's reach were arranged precision instruments for counting and measuring perforations on stamps, studying the texture of the paper, the water-mark, discovering the defects of an issue or a surcharge, checking on the colours.

Unlike the majority of his colleagues, he bought everything that came to hand, sent abroad for those packets of 500, 1,000, and 10,000 stamps which are sold to beginners and are theoretically of no value.

These stamps, despite the fact that they had passed through the hands of experienced dealers, he studied one by one, rejecting nothing out of hand, and every now and then he would make a find.

A certain issue, for example, unremarkable in its ordinary form, became a rarity when the vignette was printed from a defective block; another had been printed in the experimental stage in a colour different from the one finally selected, and the specimens of it were great rarities.

Most dealers, like most collectors, confine themselves to one period, one type of stamp.

Jonas Milk had specialized in freaks, in stamps which, for one reason or another, were out of the ordinary.

That night, magnifying glass in hand, he had worked until half past eleven. At one moment he had made up his mind to shut up the house and go and fetch his wife. Clémence and her husband lived only ten minutes away, in a quiet street leading to the canal.

He would have enjoyed walking slowly back with Gina

along the deserted pavements, even if they had found nothing to say to one another.

From fear of displeasing her, he did not carry out his project. She was quite capable of believing that he had gone out to watch over her, to make sure that she really had gone to Clémence's, or that she was coming home alone.

He went into the kitchen and lit the gas to make himself a cup of coffee, for coffee didn't prevent him from sleeping. He took the opportunity to tidy up, as his wife hadn't even put the pans away.

He didn't hold that against her either. Since his marriage the house had been dirtier than when he had lived in it alone and had managed for himself almost entirely. He did not dare tidy up or do any polishing in his wife's presence, for fear that she might take it as a reproach, but when she was not there, he always found something that needed attention.

That day, for example, it was the oven, which she had not found time to clean and which smelt of herring.

Midnight sounded from St Cecilia's Church, at the far end of the market, on the corner of the rue de Bourges. He calculated, as he had done on other occasions, that the cinema had finished at half past eleven, that it took the Reverdis barely twenty minutes to reach the rue des Deux-Ponts, that they would probably stop for a few minutes to chat with Gina.

She would not be home before half past twelve, and so, leaving one light on downstairs, he went up to the first floor, wondering whether his wife had taken a key with her. He did not remember seeing one in her hand. Usually it was almost a ritual act to slip it into her bag at the last moment.

It would only be a matter of going downstairs to open the door for her, since he wouldn't go to sleep yet. Their room had a low ceiling, with a large white-painted beam in the middle and a walnut bed, a double-fronted wardrobe with mirrors, which he had bought at the sale-room.

Even here the smell of old books came up from below mixed with the smells of the kitchen, that evening the smell of herrings.

He undressed, put on his pyjamas, and cleaned his teeth. There were two windows, and from the one giving on to the yard he could see, beyond the Chaignes' yard, the windows of the Palestris, Gina's family. They had gone to bed. Like the rest of the market people they rose before daybreak and there was no light except in the window of Gina's brother Frédo's room. Had he, perhaps, just returned from the cinema? He was a strange fellow, with his hair growing low over his forehead, his thick eyebrows, his way of looking at Jonas as if he could not forgive him for marrying his sister.

At half past twelve she hadn't come back and Milk, in bed but still wearing his glasses, was staring at the ceiling with melancholy patience.

He was not anxious yet. He might have been, for it had happened before that she did not come in, and once she had stayed away for three whole days.

On her return she had not given him any explanation. She could not have been very proud of herself, at heart. Her face was drawn, her eyes tired, she had seemed to carry an alien smell about her, but as she passed in front of him she had none the less drawn herself up to toss him a look of defiance.

He had said nothing to her. What was the use? What could he have said? On the contrary, he had been softer, more attentive than usual, and two evenings later it was she who had suggested a walk along the canal, where she had slipped her hand into his arm.

She was not a bad girl. She did not hate him, like her brother Frédo. He was convinced that she was doing her best to be a good wife, and that she was grateful to him for having married her.

Twice or three times he gave a start on hearing noises, but

it was the mice downstairs, of which he had given up trying to rid himself. All round the market, where hung such delicious smells, where so many appetizing victuals were piled, the walls were riddled with warrens forming a secret city for the rodents.

Fortunately both rats and mice found sufficient to eat outside not to be tempted to set on the books, so that Jonas no longer bothered with them. Occasionally the mice ran about the bedroom while he and Gina were in bed; they came right up to the foot of the bed as if curious to see human beings sleeping, and they had lost their fear of the human voice.

A motor-bike belonging to the young Chenu, from the fishmonger's, came to a halt on the far side of the square, then the silence returned and the church clock struck the quarter, then one o'clock, and only then did Jonas get up and go over to the straw-bottomed chair where he had laid his clothes.

The first time it had happened, he had run about the town, ashamed, searching in the dark corners, looking into the window of the only bar still open in the neighbourhood of the factory.

Today there was a possible explanation. Perhaps Poupou, Clémence's baby, was ill and Gina had stayed on to help out?

He dressed, still hoping, went downstairs, glanced into the kitchen which was empty and smelt of cold herring. He picked up his hat on his way through his office, walked out of the house locking the door behind him.

And what if Gina hadn't got a key? If she came back while he was away? If she was returning from Clémence's by another route?

He decided to turn the key in the lock once more, so that she could let herself in again. The sky was clear above the vast slate roof, with a few clouds gleaming in the moonlight. Some way off a couple were walking along the rue de Bourges and the air was so still that in spite of the distance, he could hear each remark they exchanged.

As far as the rue des Deux-Ponts he met nobody, saw only one lighted window, possibly someone waiting like him, or an invalid, someone in pain?

He was disturbed by the noise of his shoes on the pavings and it gave him the feeling of an intruder.

He knew the Reverdis' house, the second on the left after the corner, and he could see at once that there was no light on the floor the young couple occupied.

What was the use of ringing, starting a disturbance, giving rise to questions which no one could answer?

Perhaps Gina had gone back home after all. It was more than likely that she had lied, that she had not been to Clémence's, that the young couple had not been to the cinema at all.

He remembered that she had not taken a book with her as she used to do when she went to look after Poupou and it had also struck him that she took her black patent-leather bag.

For no particular reason he stood for a good five minutes on the edge of the pavement, gazing at the windows behind which there were people sleeping, then he moved off almost on tiptoe.

When he reached the Place du Vieux-Marché an enormous lorry from Moulins, the first of the day, was almost blocking the rue des Prémontrés and the driver was asleep in the cab with his mouth wide open.

In his doorway he called:

'Gina!'

As if to conjure fate, he tried to speak in a natural voice, without betraying anxiety.

'Are you there, Gina?'

He locked the door again and bolted it, hesitated whether to make a fresh cup of coffee, decided against it, and went up to his room and got back into bed.

If he slept, he was not conscious of doing so. He had left the light on for no reason and an hour went by before he removed his spectacles, without which he could see only a vague, misty world. He heard some other lorries arriving, the slamming of doors, crates and boxes being stacked on the ground.

He also heard Fernand Le Bouc opening his bar, then the first vans of the retailers.

Gina hadn't come back. Gina wouldn't be coming back.

He must have dropped off to sleep, because he didn't notice the transition from night to day. At one moment there was still a darkness pierced by the lights of the market, then suddenly there had been sunshine in the bedroom and on the bed.

With a hesitant hand he felt the place beside him, and, of course, it was empty. Usually Gina was warm, lying like a gun dog, and she had a strong feminine smell. Sometimes in her sleep she would turn over sharply and, one thigh over Jonas's thigh, press on it hard, breathing more and more heavily as she did so.

He decided not to go down, nor to get up before the right time, to follow the same routine as every other day. He did not go to sleep again and, to keep his mind occupied, he listened to the noises of the market, which he tried to identify with the same meticulousness as he applied to the scrutiny of a postage stamp.

He, too, had practically been born here. Not quite. Not like the others. But they talked to him in the mornings as they talked to one another, with the same familiar friendliness, and he had his place, so to speak, at Le Bouc's counter.

Twice he heard Ancel the butcher's voice on the pavement arguing with a man delivering some quarters of beef, and there was a row about some mutton which was fairly infuriating him. Chaigne's grocery opposite opened later, and the next house belonged to the Palestris where Angèle, Gina's mother, was already at work.

It was she who attended to the business. Louis, her husband, was a pleasant fellow, but he could not stop himself from drinking. So to keep him occupied they had bought him a three-wheeler and he delivered the orders, not only for his own shop, but for the market people who had no means of transport.

It used to humiliate him. He didn't admit it. On the one hand he was content to spend the whole day out of his house, free to drink at his leisure. But on the other hand he was no dupe, and realized that he didn't count, that he was no longer the real head of the family, and this made him drink all the more.

What ought Angèle to have done? Jonas had wondered to himself and had not found the answer.

Gina had no respect for her father. When he came to see her between errands, she would put the bottle of wine and a glass down on the table, with the words:

'There! Is that what you want?'

He would pretend to laugh, to take it as a joke. He knew it was meant seriously and yet he did not resist the need to fill his glass, though he might call out on leaving:

'You're a proper bitch!'

Jonas tried not to be present when that happened. In front of him, Palestri felt even more humiliated, and that was perhaps one of the reasons why he had nearly as big a grudge against him as his son had.

He rose at six, went down to make his coffee. He was always the first one down and in summer his first action was to open the door into the yard. Often Gina wasn't to be seen downstairs until about half past seven or eight when the shop was already open.

She liked to hang about in dressing-gown and slippers, her face glistening after her night's sleep, and it did not disturb her to be seen thus by strangers; she would go and stand on the doorstep, walk past the Chaignes' on her way to say good morning to her mother, return with vegetables or fruit.

' 'Morning, Gina!'

' 'Morning, Pierrot!'

She knew everybody, the wholesalers, the retailers, the heavy-lorry drivers as well as the country women who came to sell the produce from their gardens or their backyards. As a little girl she used to run about with bare behind between the crates and baskets.

She was no longer a little girl now. She was a woman of twenty-four and her friend Clémence had a child, while others had two or three.

She had not come home and Jonas, with careful movements, was setting down his boxes in front of the shop window, rearranging the price tickets and going over to the baker opposite to buy some croissants. He always bought five, three for himself, two for his wife, and when they automatically wrapped them up for him in brown tissue paper he did not protest.

He could easily throw away the two extra croissants and this gave him the idea of saying nothing, which, to him, meant not admitting that Gina had gone off without telling him.

Besides, had she really gone off? When she left in the evening she was only wearing her red cotton dress, only had with her her patent-leather bag.

She might come back in the course of the day, at any moment. Perhaps she was already there?

Once again he tried to conjure the fates.

'Gina!' he called, going inside, a note almost of delight in his voice.

Then he ate alone, on a corner of the kitchen table, washed up his cup, his plate, and swept up the crumbs from the croissants. To set his mind at rest he went upstairs to make sure that his wife's suitcase was still in the cupboard. She only possessed that one. The day before, when he was having his coffee at Le Bouc's, for example, she could have taken her case out of the house and left it somewhere.

The postman called and he whiled away a little time reading the post, glancing cursorily over the stamps he had ordered from Cairo.

Then all of a sudden it was ten o'clock and he went round to Fernand Le Bouc's, as he did every other morning.

'How's Gina?'

'She's all right.'

'I was wondering if she was ill. I haven't seen her this morning.'

Why hadn't he answered anything else rather than:

'*She's gone to Bourges.*'

He was angry with himself for this clumsy mistake. She might come back in half an hour, in an hour, and how would his reply be interpreted then?

A girl who sold flowers not far from the shop came rushing in to change her book, as she did every morning, for she read a novel a day.

'Is this a good one?'

He said it was. She always chose the same kind of book whose gaudy covers were a guarantee of the contents.

'Gina not here?'

'Not at the moment.'

'Is she all right?'

'Yes.'

An idea suddenly occurred to him, which made him blush, for he was ashamed of distrusting other people, of what he called evil thoughts about them. As soon as the little florist departed he went up to his room, opened the wardrobe with the mirrors, at the back of which, under his and Gina's clothes which were hanging there, he kept a steel strong-box bought at Viroulet's.

The safe was in its place and Jonas had to make an effort to go any further, take the key from his pocket, and insert it in the lock.

If Gina had returned at that moment he would have fainted for shame.

But Gina did not return and no doubt she would not be returning so soon.

The transparent envelopes containing his rarest stamps, among others the Trinidad five cents blue of 1847, with the picture of the steamer *Lady McLeod*, had vanished.

Chapter Two

He was still standing in front of the wardrobe with the mirrors, with beads of sweat on his upper lip, when he heard footsteps in the shop, then in the little room. It was rare for him to close the outside door in summer, for the house, built in depth, was ill-ventilated. Standing stock still, he waited for the male or female voice of a customer to call:

'Anyone there?'

But the steps went on into the kitchen, where the visitor waited before returning to the foot of the stairway. It was a man's step, heavy, dragging slightly, and Jonas, rooted to the spot, wondered whether the stranger was going to climb the stairs, when the harsh voice of his father-in-law grated up the staircase:

'You there, Gina?'

Why was he seized with panic, as if he had been caught out? Without shutting the steel box, he pushed the wardrobe doors to, hesitating whether to go down or let it be thought that there was nobody at home. A footstep sounded on the bottom stair. The voice called again:

'Gina!'

Only then did he stammer out:

'I'll be down in a moment.'

Before leaving the room he had time to see in the mirror that his face had reddened.

By that hour, however, Palestri was not yet drunk. Even in

the evenings he never reached the point of reeling. Early in the morning his eyes would be slightly red and bleary, and he had a tumbledown look, but after a glass or two of *marc*, or rather *grappa*, its Italian version, he was no longer entirely steady.

He did not only drink *grappa*, which Le Bouc bought especially for him, but everything he was offered or whatever he could find in the other bars where he dropped in.

When Jonas came down, his pupils were beginning to lose their lustre and his face was flushed.

'Where's Gina?' he asked, looking in the direction of the kitchen where he had expected to find her.

It surprised him as well to see his son-in-law coming down from the first floor when there was nobody downstairs, and he seemed to be waiting for some explanation. Jonas had not had the time to reflect. Just as a short while before at Fernand's, he had been caught on the wrong foot. And since he had mentioned Bourges once already, was it not better to continue?

He felt a need to defend himself, even though he had done nothing. Palestri over-awed him with roughness, his great desiccated, gnarled body standing there.

He stammered:

'She's gone to Bourges.'

He realized that he was not convincing, that his eyes, behind the thick lenses, must appear to be avoiding the other's gaze.

'To see La Loute?'

'That's what she said.'

'Did she say good-bye to her mother?'

'I don't know . . .'

Like a coward, he was retreating towards the kitchen, and as Gina used to do, took the bottle of red wine from the cupboard, put it on the wax tablecloth with a glass beside it.

'When did she go?'

Later he was to ask himself why, from that moment onwards, he acted as if he were guilty. He remembered, for example, his wife's suitcase in the cupboard. If she had gone the day before to see her friend, she would have taken the case with her. So she must have left the house that same day.

That is why he replied:

'This morning.'

Louis had stretched out his hand to the glass he had poured himself, but seemed to be hesitating suspiciously before drinking from it.

'By the 7.10 bus?'

There was only that one before the half past eleven bus, which had not yet gone through. So Jonas was forced to answer yes.

It was stupid. He was becoming caught up in a web of lies, which were bound to lead to others, and from which he would never be able to extricate himself. At seven in the morning the market was almost deserted. It was the time of the lull between the wholesalers and the ordinary customers. Gina's mother would certainly have seen her daughter passing, and in any case the girl would have gone into the shop to say good morning to her.

Other people would have seen her as well. There are some streets where people stay in their houses as if in water-tight compartments and each scarcely knows his neighbour. The Place du Vieux-Marché was different; it was rather like a barracks where the doors remained open and people knew from hour to hour what was going on in the family next door.

Why did Palestri eye his son-in-law suspiciously? Wasn't it because he looked as if he were lying? At all events he emptied his glass, in a gulp, wiped his mouth with his usual gesture, similar to that of the butcher, but did not go away immediately: he was gazing round him at the kitchen and Jonas thought he understood the reason for the contraction of his eyebrows.

There was something unnatural, that morning, in the atmosphere of the house. It was too tidy. There was nothing lying about, there was no sense of the disarray that Gina always left behind her.

' 'Bye!' he finally mumbled, heading for the door of the shop. He added, as if for his own benefit:

'I'll tell her mother she's gone. When's she coming back?'

'I don't know.'

Would it have been better for Jonas to have called him back and confessed the truth, told him that his daughter had gone off, taking his valuable stamps with her?

The ones downstairs, in the drawers of the desk, were only the common or garden stamps he bought by the packet, and the ones he had already sorted, which he was swapping or selling to schoolboys.

The strong-box, on the other hand, contained till the day before a veritable fortune, the rare stamps which he had discovered, by dint of patience and flair, over more than twenty-five years, for he had first taken an interest in stamps while at school.

One specimen alone, the pearl of his collection, a French stamp of 1849 with the head of Ceres on a bright vermilion ground, was worth, at the catalogue valuation, 600,000 francs.

The Trinidad stamp, with the steamer *Lady McLeod*, was assessed at 300,000 francs, and he possessed others of considerable value, such as the Puerto Rican two-peseta pink with the overprinted surcharge, for which he was being offered 35,000 francs.

He had never calculated the total value of his collection, but it could not have been much less than ten million francs.

The people of the Old Market had no suspicion of this wealth. He never spoke of it to anyone and he did not mind being thought a crank.

One evening, however, when one of the catalogues was lying about on the desk, Gina had begun idly turning over its pages.

'What does that mean, *double surcharge*?'

He had explained it to her.

'And *sep-ol*?'

'Sepia and olive colour.'

'And *2 p*?'

'Two pesetas.'

The abbreviations intrigued her.

'It's very complicated!' she had sighed.

She was on the point of shutting the catalogue when she had asked one last question.

'And the figure 4,000 in this column?'

'The value of the stamp.'

'You mean that stamp is worth 4,000 francs?'

He had smiled.

'Certainly.'

'Do all the figures in this column stand for the value of the stamps?'

'Yes.'

She had turned over the pages of the catalogue with renewed interest.

'Here it says 700,000. Are there really stamps worth 700,000 francs?'

'Yes.'

'Have you got one?'

'I haven't got that one, no.'

'Have you other ones as valuable?'

'Not quite.'

'Some very valuable ones?'

'Some fairly valuable.'

'Is that what you bought a steel safe for?'

This had happened the previous winter and he remembered that it was snowing outside, that he could see a white rim round the window panes. The stove was roaring in the little room. It must have been about eight o'clock in the evening.

'Goodness!'

'What?'

'Nothing. I'd never have thought it.'

In the Place du Vieux-Marché he had the reputation of having money and it would have been difficult to trace the origin of this rumour. Perhaps it was due to the fact that he had remained a bachelor for a long time? Ordinary folk naturally imagine that a bachelor puts money to one side. Apart from that, before marrying Gina, he used to eat in the restaurant, at Pepito's, another Italian, in the first house in the rue Haute, past the Grimoux-Marmion grocery, which stood on the corner of the square.

Probably for these tradespeople who were in and out of his shop all day, he seemed something of an amateur. Could anyone really make a living buying, selling, and hiring out old books? Weren't there times when an hour or even two went by without any customer going into his shop?

So, since he was alive, and since, moreover, he had a woman in two hours a day and for the whole morning on Saturdays, he must have had money.

Had Gina been disappointed that he didn't change any of his habits after marrying her? Had she been expecting a new existence?

He hadn't asked himself the question, and only now did he realize that he had been living without noticing what was happening around him.

If he looked in the drawer of the till, where he kept the money in a big wallet grey with use, would he find the right amount there? He was almost sure he would not. Gina had sometimes pilfered small amounts, rather in the manner of a child wanting to buy sweets. At first she contented herself with a few hundred-franc pieces, which she took from the drawer with the compartments where he kept the change.

Later on she had ventured to open the wallet and he had sometimes noticed that a 1,000-franc note would be missing.

Yet he gave her plenty of money for housekeeping, never refused her a new dress, underclothing, or shoes.

Perhaps at first she acted merely on a private whim, and he suspected that she had taken money in the same way from her parents' till when she lived with them. Only it must have been more difficult then, for Angèle, despite her jolly, motherly air, had a sharp eye for money. He had never mentioned it to Gina. He had thought a lot about it, and had finally come to the conclusion that it was for her brother that she stole in this way. She was five years older than he and yet people could sense an affinity between them of the kind that is normally only found between twins. There were times when one might have thought Frédo was in love with his sister, and that she reciprocated it.

It was enough for them, wherever they were, to exchange a glance to understand one another, and if Gina frowned her brother became as anxious as a lover.

Was that why he disliked Jonas? At the wedding he had been the only one not to congratulate him, and he had left right in the middle of the reception. Gina had run after him. They had whispered together a long time in the corridor of the Hôtel du Commerce where the banquet had taken place. When she came back, still dressed in white satin, it was obvious that she had been crying, and she had at once poured herself out a glass of champagne.

At the time Frédo was only seventeen. Their marriage had taken place two weeks before Clémence Ancel, their bridesmaid, had hers.

Resigned, he opened the drawer with his key, picked up the wallet and discovered to his surprise that there was not a single note missing.

It was explicable. He hadn't thought. The day before Gina had not left until after dinner and, up till the last moment, he might have had to open the cash drawer. With the stamps it was another matter, as sometimes he went a whole week without touching the steel box.

There were still some details which he did not understand, but they were material details of no great importance. For example, he always carried his keys in his trouser pocket, attached to a silver chain. When had his wife managed to get hold of them without his knowing? Not at night, because he slept more lightly than she did, and besides he was the first down in the morning. Occasionally, it was true, in order not to wake her, he would go downstairs in pyjamas and dressing-gown to make his coffee. It had not happened the day before, but the day before that, and he hadn't touched the safe since then.

'Have you got a book about bee-keeping, please?'

It was a boy about twelve years old, who had just come in, and spoken in an assured voice, his face covered in freckles, his copper-coloured hair streaked with sunlight.

'Are you thinking of keeping bees?'

'I found a swarm in a tree in the vegetable garden and my parents are going to let me make a hive, provided I do it with my own money.'

Jonas had fair ginger hair too, with freckles on the bridge of his nose. But at this child's age he must have already worn glasses as thick as the ones he was wearing now.

He had wondered to himself sometimes whether on account of his short-sightedness he saw things and people differently from others. The question intrigued him. He had read, for example, that the various species of animals do not see us as we really are, but as their eyes show us to them, and that for some we are ten times as tall, which is what makes them so timid when we approach them.

Does the same phenomenon occur with a short-sighted

person, even though his sight is more or less corrected by spectacles?

Without glasses the world was to him only a more or less luminous cloud in which floated shapes so insubstantial that he could not be sure of being able to touch them.

His spectacles, on the other hand, revealed to him the details of objects and faces as if he had been looking at them through a magnifying glass or as if they had been engraved.

Did this cause him to live in a separate sphere? Were these spectacles, without which he had to grope his way, a barrier between himself and the world outside?

In a shelf of books about animals he finally found one on bees and bee-hives.

'How about that one?'

'Is it expensive?'

He consulted, on the back cover, the pencilled price.

'A hundred francs.'

'Would you let me have it if I paid half next week?'

Jonas didn't know him. He was not from the neighbourhood. He was a country boy whose mother had probably come into the market with vegetables or poultry.

'You can take it.'

'Thank you. I will be in again next Thursday without fail.'

Outside in the sun of the street and the shade of the covered market the clientele had changed imperceptibly. Early in the morning there was a preponderance of working-class women doing their shopping after taking their children to school. It was also the time for the vans from the hotels and restaurants.

As early as nine o'clock, and especially around ten o'clock, the shoppers were better dressed, and at eleven some of them brought their maids with them to carry the parcels.

The shavings in the gutter, trampled underfoot, were losing their golden hue to turn brown and sticky, and were now becoming mixed with outer leaves of leeks, carrots, and fish heads.

Gina had taken no change of clothes with her, no under-clothes, not even a coat, though the nights were still cool.

If she had been intending to stay in the town, on the other hand, would she have had the nerve to take his most valuable stamps?

After seven o'clock in the evening, there were no more buses to Bourges, nor for anywhere else, only a train at 8.52 which connected with the Paris train, and, at 9.40, the slow train from Moulins.

The station employees knew her, but he didn't dare go and question them. It was too late. He had twice spoken of Bourges and he was obliged to stick to it.

Why had he behaved in this way? He could not account for it. It was not from fear of ridicule, because everyone, not only in the Place du Vieux-Marché, but throughout the town, knew that Gina had had many lovers before marrying him. It could not have passed unnoticed, either, that since her marriage she had had several adventures.

Was it a sort of shame that had prompted him to reply, first to Le Bouc, then to Palestri:

'She has gone to Bourges'?

Shame which was born of shyness? What happened between him and Gina did not concern anybody else, and he believed himself to be the last person to have any right to discuss it.

But for the disappearance of the stamps he would have waited all day, then all night, hoping from one moment to the next to see her return like a dog which has run away.

The room upstairs had not been done, and the strong-box had not been closed, so he went up, made his bed as meticulously as when he was a bachelor and the maid was away.

It was as a maid that Gina had come into the house. Before her there had been another, old Léonie, who at the age of seventy still put in her eight or nine hours a day with different employers. In the end her legs had swollen up. Latterly she could hardly manage to climb the stairs, and as her children, who lived in Paris, did not care to look after her, Dr Joublin had put her in a home.

For a month Jonas had been without anyone, and it didn't worry him unduly. He knew Gina, like everyone else, through having seen her pass by, or from selling her an occasional book. At that time she had behaved in a provocative manner with him as she used to with all men, and he blushed every time she came into his shop, especially in summer, when it seemed to him that she left behind her a trace of the smell of her armpits.

'Haven't you got anyone yet?' Le Bouc had asked him one morning when he was having his coffee in the little bar.

He had never understood why Le Bouc and the others from the Square did not use the familiar '*tu*' with him, for they nearly all used it among themselves, calling one another by their Christian names.

They didn't call him Milk, however, almost as if it were not his name, nor Monsieur Milk, but, nearly always, Monsieur Jonas.

And yet at the age of two he was living in the Square, just next door to Ancel's, the butcher's, and it was his father who had converted the fishmonger's, '*À La Marée*', now kept by the Chenus.

It was not because he had not been to the communal school either, like most of them, but to a private school, then to the *lycée*. The proof was that they were already addressing his father before him as Monsieur Constantin.

Fernand had asked him:

'Haven't you got anybody yet?'

He had replied no, and Le Bouc had leant over his counter.

'You ought to have a word or two with Angèle.'

He had been so surprised that he had asked, as if there could have been two Angèles:

29

'The greengrocer?'

'Yes. She's having trouble with Gina. She can't do anything with her. I think she wouldn't be sorry to see her working outside so that someone else could break her in.'

Up till then Gina had been more or less helping her mother in the shop, and slipping off at every opportunity.

'You wouldn't like to talk to her yourself?' Jonas had suggested.

It seemed to him incongruous, indecent almost, on his part, as a bachelor, although he had no ulterior motives, to go and ask a woman like Angèle to let him have her daughter for three hours a day.

'I'll have a word with her father. No! I'd better see Angèle. I'll give you her reply tomorrow.'

To his great surprise, the reply next day was yes, or as good as yes, and he was almost frightened by it. Angèle had told Le Bouc, to be precise:

'Tell that Jonas I'll come round and see him.'

She had come, late one afternoon during a slack period, had insisted on seeing over the house, and had discussed wages.

That meant changing his habits, and it was not without reluctance that he gave up going at half past twelve and sitting in Pepito's little restaurant, where he had his own pigeon-hole for his table-napkin and his bottle of mineral water.

'After all, if she's going to work at all, it might as well be worth her while. It's high time she got down to some cooking, and we hardly have time in our place at midday to eat more than a piece of sausage or some cheese.'

Didn't Gina resent his having engaged her, at first? Anyone would have thought she was doing everything possible to make herself unbearable so that he would throw her out.

After a week with him she was working from nine o'clock in the morning until one. Then Angèle had decided:

'It's absurd to cook for one person alone. It costs no more to do it for two. She might just as well have lunch with you and do the washing-up before leaving.'

Suddenly his life had changed. He didn't know everything, because he didn't hear the gossip, perhaps also because people didn't speak freely in front of him. He didn't understand, at first, why Gina was always in low spirits and why she would suddenly turn aggressive only, soon afterwards, to burst into tears in the middle of her housework.

It was then three months since Marcel Jenot had been arrested and Jonas hardly ever read the papers. He had heard his name mentioned at Le Bouc's, for it had created quite a sensation. Marcel Jenot, the son of a dressmaker who worked for most of the women of the market, including the Palestris, was under-cook at the Commercial Hotel, the best and most expensive in town. Jonas must have seen him at some time or other without paying any attention. His photograph, in the papers, showed a young man with a high forehead and a serious expression with, however, a rather disquieting curl to his lip.

At twenty-one he had just finished his military service in Indo-China and was once more living with his mother in the rue des Belles-Feuilles, the street beyond Pepito's restaurant.

Like most young men of his age he owned a motor-cycle. One evening on the Saint-Amand road, a large car-load of Parisians had been stopped by a motor-cyclist who seemed to be asking for help and then, brandishing an automatic, had demanded money from the occupants, after which he had punctured the four tyres of the car and made off.

The motor-cycle's number plate, at the time of the hold-up, was covered with a layer of black paint. How had the police managed to trace it to Marcel? The papers must have explained it, but Jonas didn't know.

The investigation was under way when Gina had gone into service with him, and a month later the trial had taken place at Montluçon.

It was Le Bouc who had told the bookseller about it.

'How is Gina?'

'She does her best.'

'Not too upset?'

'Why?'

'Marcel is being tried next week.'

'Which Marcel?'

'The one in the hold-up. It's her boy friend.'

She actually had to stay away for a few days and when she came back to resume work, it was a long time before she opened her mouth.

That had been nearly three years ago now. A year after she had joined him as a housemaid Jonas married her, surprised at what was happening to him. He was thirty-eight and she twenty-two. Even when, in the sunlight, her body almost naked under her dress, she used to move to and fro around him and he breathed her smell, he had never made a single ambiguous gesture.

At Le Bouc's they had adopted the habit of asking him, with a smile at the corner of the mouth:

'Well, well! And how's Gina?'

He would reply, naïvely:

'She's very well.'

Some of them went so far as to give him a wink, which he would pretend not to see, and others seemed to suspect him of keeping something up his sleeve.

By keeping his ears pricked and asking a few questions here and there, he could easily have found out the names of all the lovers Gina had had since she had begun to knock about with men at the age of thirteen. He could also have found out about what had happened between her and Marcel. He was not unaware that she had been questioned several times by the police in the course of the inquiry and that Angèle had been summoned by the magistrate.

What would be the use? It was not in his character. He had always lived alone, without imagining that he would one day be able to live otherwise.

Gina did not keep house as well as old Léonie. Her table-cloths, when she took the trouble to use them, were seldom clean and, if she sometimes sang as she worked, there were days when her face remained set, her mouth truculent.

Often, in the middle of the morning, she would disappear on the pretext of doing some shopping up the road and come back, with no apology, two hours later.

Even so, hadn't her presence in the house become essential to Jonas? Had there been a conspiracy, as some people claimed, to force his hand?

One afternoon Angèle had called in the clothes she always wore during the day in her shop, for she only really dressed up on Sundays.

'Well now, Jonas!'

She was one of the few people not to call him Monsieur Jonas. True, she addressed most of the customers in the most familiar manner.

'Don't touch those pears, love!' she would shout at Dr Martroux's wife, one of the most prim and proper women in the town. 'When I go to see your husband I don't play with his instruments.'

That day she strode into the kitchen and sat down on a chair.

'I've come to tell you I've had an offer for my daughter.'

Her gaze made an inventory of the room, where nothing can have escaped her attention.

'Some people from Paris who have just settled in the town. The husband, an engineer, has been appointed assistant manager of the factory and they are looking for someone. It's a good post, and Gina would get board and lodging. I promised them a reply the day after tomorrow. You can think it over.'

He had had twenty-four hours of panic and had turned the

question over in his mind in all its aspects again and again . . .
As a bachelor he couldn't have a living-in maid. Besides, there
was only one bedroom in the house. That Angèle knew. So
why had she come to offer him a sort of first refusal?

It was difficult enough to keep Gina in the house all day for
she would have nothing to do for hours on end.

Had Angèle thought of all this?

During this time Gina seemed to be unaware of what was
going on and behaved in her normal way.

They always had lunch together, in the kitchen, opposite
one another, she with her back to the oven, from where she
reached for the pots as she needed them, without having to
get up.

'Gina!'

'Yes.'

'There's something I want to ask you.'

'What?'

'You promise to answer me frankly?'

He could still see her clearly as he pronounced these words,
but the next moment she was nothing more than a wraith
before his eyes, for his spectacles had suddenly misted over.

'Aren't I always frank?'

'Yes.'

'Usually I get criticized for being too frank.'

'Not by me.'

'What do you want to ask?'

'Do you like the house?'

She looked round her with what seemed to him like indifference. 'I mean,' he persisted, 'would you like to live here
altogether?'

'Why do you ask me that?'

'Because I should be happy if you would accept.'

'Accept what?'

'Becoming my wife.'

If there had been a plot, Gina was not in on it, for she exclaimed with a nervous laugh:

'Don't be silly!'

'I'm serious.'

'You'd marry me?'

'That's what I am suggesting.'

'*Me?*'

'You.'

'You realize what sort of a girl I am?'

'I think I know you as well as anybody else.'

'In that case you're a brave man.'

'What's your answer?'

'My answer's that you're very kind, but that it's impossible.'

There was a splash of sunlight on the table and it was on this that Jonas fastened his gaze, rather than on the young girl's face.

'Why?'

'Because.'

'You don't want me?'

'I didn't say that, Monsieur Jonas. You are certainly very decent. In fact you're the only man who never tried to take advantage of the situation. Even Ancel himself, though he's the father of one of my friends, took me into the shed in his backyard when I was only fifteen. I could name nearly all of them, one by one, and you would be amazed. To start with I wondered when you were going to pluck up courage.'

'Do you think you couldn't be happy here?'

Then she made her frankest reply:

'It would be peaceful, at any rate.'

'Well, that's something, isn't it?'

'Yes, of course. Only supposing we didn't get on together? Better not say any more about it. I'm not the kind of girl to make a man like you happy.'

'It's not me that counts.'

'Who does then?'

'You.'

He was sincere. He was so overcome with tenderness while he was talking about this subject, that he didn't dare move from fear of allowing his emotion to break out.

'Me and happiness . . .' she said bitterly, between her clenched teeth.

'Let's say peace, as you called it yourself.'

She had glanced at him sharply.

'Was it my mother who suggested it to you? I knew she'd been to see you, but . . .'

'No. She only told me you were being offered a better job.'

'My mother has always wanted to get me out of the way.'

'Won't you think it over?'

'What's the point?'

'Wait at any rate until tomorrow before giving me a definite answer, will you?'

'If you insist!'

That day she had broken a plate while she was doing the washing-up, and as had happened now, two years later, she had gone off forgetting to clean the stove.

At about four o'clock in the afternoon, as usual, Jonas had gone for his cup of coffee at Le Bouc's and Fernand had watched him closely.

'Is it true, what they're saying?'

'What are they saying?'

'That you are going to marry Gina.'

'Who told you that?'

'Louis, just now. He had a quarrel with Angèle over it.'

'Why?'

Le Bouc had looked uncomfortable.

'They don't have the same ideas.'

'He's against it?'

'I'll say!'

'Why?'

Louis had certainly given a reason, but Le Bouc did not pass it on.

'You never can tell just what's going on in his head,' he replied evasively.

'Is he angry?'

'He talked about going and knocking your block off. That won't stop him doing what Angèle decides. It makes no difference him protesting, he's got no say in his house.'

'And Gina?'

'You must know what she said to you better than I do. The most difficult of all will be her brother.'

'Why?'

'I don't know. It's just a hunch. He's a strange lad, with ideas all his own.'

'He doesn't like me?'

'Apart from his sister he probably likes nobody. She's the only one who can stop him making a fool of himself. A month ago he wanted to join up in Indo-China.'

'She didn't want him to?'

'He's only a boy. He's never been anywhere. As soon as he got there he would be even more unhappy than he is here.'

A customer was going into the shop, near by, and Jonas made for the door.

'See you soon.'

'Good luck!'

He had slept badly, that night. At eight o'clock Gina had come in to start work without speaking, without looking at him, and he had waited a long quarter of an hour before questioning her.

'Have you got the answer?'

'Do you really mean it?'

'Yes.'

'You won't hold it against me later?'

37

'I promise.'

She had shrugged her shoulders.

'In that case it's as you wish.'

It was so unexpected that it made him empty of all emotion. He looked at her dumbfounded, without daring to approach, without taking her hand, and even less did it occur to him to kiss her.

Afraid of having misunderstood her, he insisted:

'You are consenting to marry me?'

She was sixteen years younger than he and yet it was she who had looked at him as if he were a child, a protective smile at her lips.

'Yes.'

So as not to betray himself in front of her, he had gone up to his room and, before leaning out of the window, had stood for a long while in a trance in front of one of the wardrobe mirrors. It was in May. A shower had just fallen but the sun was shining again and making great bright patches on the wet tiles of the immense roof. There was a market, like today, and he had gone out to buy strawberries, the first of the season.

A big, strong woman, dressed in black, a blue apron round her middle, was entering his shop in an authoritative manner and casting a great shadow. It was Angèle, whose hand always smelt of leeks.

'Is it true what Louis tells me? What's she gone to Bourges for?'

He was smaller than she was and a great deal less powerful. He stammered:

'I don't know.'

'Did she take the bus this morning?'

'Yes.'

'Without coming to see me?'

She, too, was looking at him suspiciously.

'Was there a quarrel between the two of you?'

'No.'

'Answer me like a man, for God's sake! What's gone wrong?'

'Nothing . . .'

She had begun to address him familiarly the day of the engagement, but Louis had never been willing to follow her example.

'*Nothing! Nothing!* . . .' she mimicked. 'You ought at least to be capable of preventing your wife from running away. When did she promise to come back?'

'She didn't say.'

'That's better than ever!'

She seemed to flatten him with a look, with all her vigorous bulk, and then, turning sharply on her heel to leave, she ground out:

'Little rat!'

Chapter Three

His first impulse had been to go and buy a slice of ham, or some cold meat, from Pascal, the butcher on the other side of the market, just at the beginning of the rue du Canal, or even not to eat at all, or perhaps to make do with the two extra croissants he had been given that morning. He ought not to have taken them. That did not fit in with the supposed departure of Gina for Bourges. Strictly he would only have needed to buy three croissants.

It was not on his own account that he was so distraught, out of self-respect or fear of what people would say.

It was on her account. Her theft of his stamps, which were all he cared about in the world apart from her, made no difference: he considered it his duty to defend her.

He did not know yet what against. He had been a prey, particularly since that morning, to a vague uneasiness which almost prevented him from thinking about his own distress. In time, every one of his feelings would doubtless detach themselves more clearly and he would be able to single them out. For the moment, stunned, he was dealing with the immediate problems first, in the belief that by acting in this way it was Gina he was protecting.

On the rare occasions when she had visited La Loute and had spent the whole day at Bourges, he had returned to his bachelor habits and eaten at Pepito's. This, then, was what he had to do today, and when, at noon, the bell announcing the end of the market pealed out into the sunlight, vibrating like a convent bell, he began to bring the boxes of books indoors.

Already the refuse lorry was advancing yard by yard round the square, while five men loaded on to it everything they could shovel up out of the gutter. Many of the market women, especially the ones from the country, had already left, and some, before taking their bus, were eating the snacks they had brought with them, at Le Bouc's or the Trianon Bar.

It went against the grain to leave the house, rather as if he were betraying something, and, against all evidence, he told himself that Gina would perhaps return while he was away.

The rue Haute was a narrow, gently sloping street, despite its name, and formed the main artery of the most densely populated neighbourhood. The shops in it were more varied than elsewhere. American surplus stores and cheap jewellery were sold in it, and there were at least three junk shops and old-clothes stores.

Since the chemical products factory had been installed a kilometre away, it had become a sort of Italian quarter at the far end, which some people actually called Little Italy. As the factory grew in importance, workers had come from elsewhere, first of all Poles, who had installed themselves a little farther up, then at the end, almost outside the factory gates, a few families of Algerians.

Pepito's restaurant, with the olive-coloured walls and the crinkled paper cloths, had nevertheless preserved its peaceful character and, at midday, the same habitués were to be found there, who, as Jonas had done for such a long time, took their meals there year in year out.

Marie, the *patron*'s wife, did the cooking while her husband ran the bar and their niece waited at table.

'Why, Monsieur Jonas!' the little Italian cried out on catching sight of him. 'What a pleasant surprise to see you!'

Then, afraid suddenly that he had committed a gaffe to appear so pleased:

'Gina's not ill, I trust?'

And he had to repeat his old refrain:

'She's gone to Bourges.'

'Well, we all have to change our routine now and again. There, your old table's free. Julia! Lay a place for Monsieur Jonas.'

It was probably here that Jonas became most aware of the vacuum which had just been created in his life. For years Pepito's restaurant, where nothing had changed, had been a second home for him. Yet, here he was, feeling out of place, seized with panic at the idea that he might have to return every day.

The Widower was in his place, and seemed almost to be on the point of welcoming Jonas with the batting of his eyelids which in the old days had served as a greeting.

They had never spoken to one another. For years, they had occupied two tables opposite one another by the window, and they used to arrive at more or less the same time.

Jonas knew his name, through Pepito. He was Monsieur Métras, chief clerk at the Town Hall, but in his mind he always labelled him the Widower.

He had never known Madame Métras, who had died fifteen years before. As there were no children in the family, the husband, left to his own devices, had taken to having his meals at Pepito's.

He must have been fifty-five years old, perhaps more. He was a tall man, very broadly built, thick and hard, with iron grey hair, bushy eyebrows and darker hair sprouting from his nostrils and ears. His complexion was greyish as well, and Jonas had never seen him smile. He didn't read the paper as he ate, like most single diners, never joined in a conversation with anybody, and chewed his food carefully, gazing straight to his front.

Many months had passed before they batted eyelids at one

another in greeting, and Jonas was the only person to whom the Widower had ever made this concession.

A diminutive, asthmatic dog, fat and almost impotent, used to sit under the table; it could not have been far off twenty years old, for it had once been Madame Métras's dog.

The Widower used to go and fetch it from his flat on coming out of his office, and take it to the restaurant where they gave it its food. Then he led it off again, slowly, waiting while it relieved itself before returning to the Town Hall, and in the evening the performance was repeated.

Why, while Jonas was eating, did the Widower watch him today more closely than before? It wasn't possible that he already knew. Yet anyone would have sworn that he was thinking to himself, restraining a snigger:

'Ah! So, you're back again!'

Rather as if the two of them had been members of the same club, as if Jonas had left it for a time and finally come back, repentant, to the fold.

All this existed only in his imagination, but what was not imagination was his terror at the idea of once again sitting opposite the chief clerk every day.

'What will you have for dessert, Monsieur Jonas? There's éclairs and apple tart.'

He had always liked pudding, particularly apple tart, which he chose, and he felt guilty at yielding to his greed at such a moment.

'What's your news, Monsieur Jonas?'

Pepito was tall like Palestri, dry and lean, but unlike his compatriot he was always smiling and affable. Anyone would have thought running a restaurant was all a game for him, he did it with such good humour. Maria, his wife, had become enormous as a result of living in a kitchen six yards square, but that did not prevent her remaining young and alluring. She, too, was jolly and would burst into laughter over nothing.

As they had no children, they had adopted a nephew whom they had had sent over from their country and who could be seen doing his homework in the evening at one of the restaurant tables.

'How's Gina?'

'She's all right.'

'The other day my wife met her in the market and, I don't know why, she got the impression that she was expecting a baby. Is that true?'

He said no, almost ashamed, for he was sure it was his fault if Gina was not pregnant.

What had misled Maria was that recently Gina had taken to eating more than usual, with a sort of frenzy, and from being plump as she was before, had become fat to the extent of needing to alter her clothes.

At first he had rejoiced at her appetite, for in the early days of their marriage she hardly ate at all. He used to encourage her, seeing it as a sign of contentment, thinking that she was acclimatizing herself to their life, and that she might end by actually feeling happy.

He had said so to her and she had replied with a vague, rather protective smile, which she turned on him increasingly often now. She had not her mother's authoritative personality, quite the opposite. She did not concern herself with business, or money, or the decisions that had to be taken in household matters.

Yet, despite the difference in age, it was she who adopted an indulgent manner now and then towards Jonas.

He was her husband and she treated him as such. But in her eyes, perhaps, he was not quite a man, a real male, and she seemed to look on him as a backward child.

Had he been wrong not to have been more severe with her? Ought he to have taken her in hand? Would that have changed matters?

He had no desire to think about it. The Widower, opposite, was hypnotizing him and he finished up his apple tart faster than he would have wished, in order to escape his gaze.

'So soon?' exclaimed Pepito when he asked for the bill. 'Aren't you going to have your coffee?'

He would take it at Le Bouc's, with the possibility in the back of his mind of hearing some news there. In the old days he used to eat as slowly as Monsieur Métras, and the majority of single men who lunched in the restaurant and who, for the most part, chatted with the *patron* afterwards.

'Julia! Monsieur Jonas's bill.'

And, addressing him:

'Shall we be seeing you this evening?'

'Perhaps.'

'She hasn't gone for long?'

'I don't know yet.'

It was starting all over again. He was floundering, no longer knowing what to reply to the questions that were being put to him, realizing that it would be worse tomorrow and worse still in the days to follow.

What would happen, for example, if La Loute came to see her family and disclosed that Gina had not been to Bourges? It was unlikely, but he was envisaging everything. The woman everyone called La Loute was really Louise Hariel, and her parents kept the grain store in the market, just opposite Jonas, on the other side of the great roof.

He had seen her, in the same way as he had seen Gina, running about among the crates when she was not yet ten. At that time, with her round face, her blue eyes with long lashes and her curly hair, she looked like a doll. It was odd, for her father was a thin, plain little man and her mother in the drab background of the grain store, which faced north and never got the sun, looked like a dried-up old spinster.

The two Hariels, man and wife, wore the same grey smocks

45

and, from living together, each behind their own counter, making the same movements, they had ended by resembling one another.

La Loute had been the only one of the girls of the Square to be educated in a convent, which she had not left until the age of seventeen. She was also the best-dressed and her clothes were very lady-like. On Sundays when she went to High Mass with her parents, everyone used to turn round, and the mothers held up her deportment as an example to their daughters.

For about two years she had worked as a secretary to the Privas Press, a business which had been flourishing for three generations, then, all of a sudden, it had been put about that she had found a better job in Bourges.

Her parents didn't mention the subject. The two of them were the most cantankerous shopkeepers in the Old Market and many customers preferred to go all the way to the rue de la Gare for their purchases.

La Loute and Gina were good friends. With Clémence, the butcher's daughter, they had for long been an inseparable trio.

At first people had said that La Loute was working with an architect in Bourges, then with a bachelor doctor with whom she had lived on marital terms.

Various people had met her there, and there was talk of her expensive tastes, her fur coat. The latest news was that she had a baby Citroën, which had been seen outside her parents' door one evening.

La Loute had not spent the night with them. The neighbours claimed to have heard raised voices, which was strange, for the Hariels hardly ever opened their mouths and someone had actually called them the two fish.

To Jonas, Gina had contented herself with saying, on one of her returns from Bourges:

'She leads her life as best she can and it's not easy for anyone.'

After a moment's reflection she had added:

'Poor girl. She's too kind.'

Why too kind? Jonas had not inquired. He recognized that it was none of his business, that it was women's and even girls' gossip, that friends like Clémence, La Loute and Gina, when they got together, became schoolgirls again and had a right to their own secrets.

Another time, Gina had said:

'It's all plain sailing for some people.'

Was she referring to Clémence, who had a young husband, a good-looking fellow, and who had had the finest wedding in the Old Market?

He himself wasn't young, nor a good-looking fellow, and all he had been able to offer was security. Had Gina really wanted security, *peace*, as he had said the first day?

Where was she at that moment, with the stamps which she imagined she could sell without difficulty? Surely she could have had hardly any money on her, even if, without Jonas's knowledge, she had put some aside for the occasion? Her brother could not have given her anything either, because it was she who slipped him money from time to time.

Because she had seen the prices in the catalogue she had told herself that she had only to call at any stamp dealer, in Paris or anywhere else, to sell them. It was true of certain of them, the ones only comparatively rare, but it was not the case for the valuable ones, like the 1849 Ceres.

Stamp dealers, like diamond merchants, form a sort of confraternity throughout the world, and are more or less known to one another. They know, usually, in whose hands such and such a rare stamp is, and watch for a chance to acquire it for their customers.

At least five of the stamps she had taken were known in this way. If she were to offer them for sale at any reputable dealers there was a good chance that the assistant would detain her on some pretext and telephone the police.

She was in no danger of being put into prison, because she was his wife and theft is not recognized between married people. Even so they would start an inquiry and they would get in touch with him.

Would it be in this way, on account of her ignorance, that her escapade would come to an end?

He was not sure he would wish that. He didn't wish it. It hurt him to think of Gina's shame, her discomfiture, her rage.

Wouldn't it be still worse if she were to entrust the sale to someone else? By now she was no longer alone, on that score he had no illusions. And this time it was not a question of some young male from the town whom she had not been able to resist following for a night or two.

She had set off deliberately and her departure had been premeditated, organized at least twenty-four hours in advance. In other words he had lived with her for twenty-four hours without realizing that it was probably the last day they would spend together.

He was walking along the street now, with slow steps, and the bare space under the tile roof seemed immense, given over to a few men who were hosing it down and scrubbing the cement flooring with brooms. Most of the shops were shut until two o'clock.

He was shrinking from the moment of going into Le Bouc's to drink his coffee, for he didn't feel like speaking to anybody, least of all to answer any more questions. He was devoid of hatred, or bitterness. What was filling his heart was a sad, anxious, and almost serene tenderness, and he stopped for a good minute watching two puppies, one of them lying on its back in the sun, with its four paws waving in the air, playing at biting each other.

He remembered the smell of herrings in the kitchen, the oven which Gina in her haste had not washed and to which bits of fish were sticking. He tried to remember what they had found to talk about at that last meal, but could not do so. Then he tried to recall the minute details of the day before, which he had spent like an ordinary day, when it was really the most important one in his life.

One image came back to him: he was behind his counter, serving an old gentleman who didn't know exactly what he wanted when Gina, who had gone up a little earlier than usual to do her face, had come down in her red dress. It was one of last year's dresses, and this was the first time he had seen it this season; because Gina had put on weight it clung more closely than ever to her body.

She had gone over to the doorway and into the triangle of sunlight, and he could never remember having seen her looking so lovely.

He hadn't told her so because, when he paid her a compliment, she would shrug her shoulders irritably and sometimes her face would cloud over.

Once she had countered, almost dryly:

'Forget it! I'll be an old woman soon enough, for God's sake!'

He thought he understood. He had no wish to analyse the matter any further. Obviously she meant that she was losing her youth in this old house which smelt of mouldering paper. It was doubtless an ironic way of reassuring him, of letting him know that they would soon be on equal terms and that he would no longer need to be afraid.

'I'm going to go and say good morning to Mama,' she had told him.

Usually, at that hour, her visits to her mother's shop didn't last for long, for Angèle, harassed with customers, had no time to waste. But Gina had been absent for nearly an hour. When she had come back, she didn't come from the right, but from the left, in other words from the opposite direction to the house of her parents, and yet she was not carrying any parcels.

She never received any letters, it suddenly struck him. Not counting La Loute, she had several married friends who no longer lived in the town. Oughtn't she to have received at least a postcard from them now and again?

The Post Office was in the rue Haute, five minutes from Pepito's. Did she have her mail sent there poste restante? Or had she been to make a telephone call from the box?

During the two years they had been married she had never mentioned Marcel, who had been sentenced to five years in prison. When she had gone off on her escapades, it was perforce with other men, which had led Jonas to suppose that she had forgotten about Jenot.

It was at least six months since she had gone out in the evening on her own, except to look after Clémence's baby, and each time she had returned punctually. Besides, if she had seen a man, he would have noticed, for she was not a woman on whom love left no mark. He knew the look on her face when she had been with a man, her slack, shifty manner, and even the smell of her body which was not the same.

Madame Hariel, the grain seller, stood behind her shop door with the handle removed, her pale face pressed to the glass panel, watching him as he wandered along the pavement like a man who does not know where he is going, and he finally headed in the direction of Le Bouc's bar. The latter was still at lunch with his wife at the back of the café, and they were finishing their black pudding.

'Don't move,' he said. 'I've plenty of time.'

It was the slack time of the day. Fernand, before having his lunch, had swept up the dirty sawdust and the red floor stones shone brightly, the house smelt of cleanliness.

'Did you have lunch at Pepito's?'

He nodded. Le Bouc had a bony face, and used to wear a blue apron. Except on Sundays and two or three times at the cinema, Jonas had never seen him in a coat.

With his mouth full, he said as he went over to the percolator:

'Louis asked me just now if I had seen Gina go past and I said I hadn't. He was having one of his bad bouts. It's a pity that a fine chap like him can't stop himself from drinking.'

Jonas unwrapped his two lumps of sugar and held them in his hand, while waiting for his cup of coffee. He liked the smell of Le Bouc's bar, even though it was loaded with alcohol, just as he liked the smell of old books which reigned in his own house. He liked the smell of the market as well, especially during the fresh fruit season, and he sometimes strolled about among the stalls to breathe it in, at the same time keeping an eye on his bookshop from afar.

Le Bouc had just said, referring to Louis:

'A fine chap . . .'

And Jonas noticed for the first time that it was an expression he often used. Ancel was a fine chap as well, and Benaiche the police constable, for whom the retailers filled a crate of provisions every morning, which his wife came to fetch at nine o'clock.

Angèle, too, despite her shrewish temperament, was a fine woman.

Everybody, around the market, except perhaps for the Hariels, who shut themselves up in their own house as if to avoid God knows what contagion, greeted one another each morning with good humour and cordiality. Everybody also worked hard and respected hard work in others.

Of Marcel, when the hold-up affair had come to light, they had said pityingly:

'It's funny. Such a nice lad . . .'

Then they had added:

'It must be Indo-China that did it to him. That's no place for young lads.'

If they spoke of La Loute and the mysterious life she led at Bourges, they didn't hold that against her either.

'Girls today aren't what they used to be. Education's changed too.'

As for Gina, she remained one of the most popular figures in the market, and when she passed by with a sway of her hips, a smile on her lips, her teeth sparkling, their faces would light up. They all followed her latest adventures. She had been seen one evening, when she was hardly seventeen, lying with a lorry driver on the back of a lorry.

'Hullo there, Gina!' they used to call out to her.

And no doubt they envied the good fortune of the men who had slept with her. Many of them had tried. Some had succeeded. Nobody held it against her for being what she was. They were nearer to being grateful, for without her the Vieux-Marché would not have been quite what it was.

'Is it true that she took the morning bus?' asked Le Bouc, returning to his place at the table.

As Jonas made no reply, he took his silence to mean that he was correct and went on:

'In that case, she will have been with my niece, Gaston's daughter, who's gone to see a new specialist.'

Jonas knew her. She was a young girl with a pretty but anaemic face who had a deformed hip and in order to walk had to thrust the right-hand side of her body forward. She was seventeen years old.

Since the age of twelve, she had been in the hands of specialists, who had made her undergo various courses of treatment. She had been operated on two or three times without any appreciable success and, at about the age of fifteen, she had spent an entire year in plaster.

She remained sweet and cheerful and her mother came several times a week to change books for her, sentimental novels which she chose carefully herself, out of fear that one of the characters might have been crippled as she was.

'Is her mother with her?'

'No. She went by herself. Gina will have kept her company.'

'Is she coming back this evening?'

'On the five o'clock bus.'

So, then, they would know that Gina had not gone to Bourges. What would he say to Louis when he came to demand an explanation?

For the Palestri family would certainly want explanations from him. They had entrusted their daughter to him, and considered him henceforth responsible for her.

Incapable of looking after her, living in fear of a scandal which might at any moment break out, Angèle had thrust her into his arms. It was that, to put it bluntly, that she had come to do when she had talked to him about a place for her daughter with the assistant manager of the factory. The story may have been true, but she had taken advantage of it.

Even now he was grateful to her for it, for his life without Gina had had no flavour; it was a little as if he had not lived before.

What intrigued him was what had happened in the Palestri family during that period. That there had been discussions there was no question. Frédo's attitude was not in any doubt either, and he must have argued with his parents that they were pushing his sister into the arms of an old man.

But Louis? Did he, too, prefer to see his daughter chasing men than married to Jonas?

'It looks as if we're in for a hot summer. That's what the almanack says, anyway. Storms next week.'

He wiped his spectacles which the steam of his coffee had misted over, and stood there for a moment like an owl in the sun, blinking his pink eyelids. It was rare for him to take off his glasses in public; he didn't know exactly why he had done so, for he had never found himself in this position before. It gave him a sense of inferiority, rather as when one dreams that one is stark naked or trouserless in the middle of a crowd.

Gina used to see him like this every day and perhaps that

was why she treated him differently from the others. His thick lenses, not rimmed with metal or tortoise-shell, worked both ways. While they enabled him to observe the minutest details of the world outside, they enlarged his pupils for other people and gave them a fixed look, a hardness which in reality they did not possess.

Once, standing in his doorway, he had heard a small boy who was passing say to his mother:

'Hasn't that man got large eyes!'

Actually his eyes weren't large. It was the glasses which gave them a globular appearance.

'See you later,' he sighed, after counting out his coins and putting them on the counter.

'See you later. Good afternoon.'

At around five o'clock Le Bouc would close his bar, for in the afternoon few customers came. If he stayed open it was mainly for the convenience of his neighbours. The day before a market he would go to bed at eight in the evening so as to be up at three next morning.

Tomorrow, Friday, there was no market. Every other day, four days in the week to be precise, the space beneath the tiled roof stood empty and served as a parking place for cars and a playground for children.

For the last two or three weeks, the children were to be seen charging about on roller skates which made a screeching sound for miles around, then, as if they had been given the word, they changed their game and took up skittles, spinning-tops, or yo-yos. It followed a rhythm, like the seasons, only more mysterious, for it was impossible to tell where the decision came from and the vendor at the bazaar in the rue Haute was taken by surprise every time.

'I want a kite, please.'

He would sell ten, twenty, in the space of two days, order others and then only sell one for the rest of the year.

Taking his keys from his pocket reminded Jonas of the steel strong-box and Gina's departure. He encountered the smell of the house again, and the atmosphere was stale, now that the sun no longer fell on its front. He took out the two book-boxes, mounted on legs with castors, then stood in the middle of the shop, not knowing what to do with himself.

Yet he had spent many years like this, alone, and had never suffered from it. Had not even noticed that there was something missing.

What did he do in the old days, at this time? He sometimes would read, behind the counter. He had read a great deal, not only novels, but works on the most varied subjects, sometimes the most unexpected ones, ranging from political economy to the report of an archaeological excavation. Everything interested him. He would pick out at random a book on mechanics, for example, thinking only to glance over a couple of pages, and then read it from cover to cover. He had read in this way, from the first page to the last, *The History of the Consulate and the Empire*, as he had read, before selling them to a lawyer, twenty-one-odd volumes of nineteenth-century trials.

He particularly liked works on geography, ones following a region from its geological formation right up to its economic and cultural expansion.

His stamps acted as reference marks. The names of countries, sovereigns, and dictators, did not evoke in his mind a brightly coloured map or photograph, but a delicate vignette enclosed in a transparent packet.

It was in this way, rather than through literature, that he came to know Russia, where he had been born forty years before.

His parents were living in Archangel at the time, right at the top of the map, on the White Sea, where five sisters and a brother had been born before him.

Of the entire family he was the only one not to know Russia, which he had left at the age of one. Maybe this was why at school he had begun to collect stamps. He must have been thirteen when one of his classmates had shown him his album.

'Look!' he had said to him. 'There's a picture of your country.'

It was, he could remember all the better now that he possessed the stamp along with many other Russian ones, a 1905 blue and pink with a picture of the Kremlin.

'I've got some other ones, you know, but they're portraits.'

The stamps, issued in 1913 for the third centenary of the Romanovs, depicted Peter I, Alexander II, Alexis Michaelovitch, Paul I.

Later he was to make a complete collection of them, including the Winter Palace and the wooden palace of the Boyar Romanovs.

His eldest sister Alyosha, who was sixteen when he was born, would now be fifty-six – if she were still alive. Nastasia would be fifty-four and Daniel, his only brother, who died in infancy, would have been just fifty.

The other three sisters, Stéphanie, Sonia, and Doussia, were forty-eight, forty-five, and forty-two and, because he was the nearest to her in age, also because of her name, it was of Doussia that he thought most often.

He had never seen their faces. He didn't know anything about them, whether they were dead or alive, if they had rallied to the party or been massacred.

The manner of his departure from Russia had been typical of his mother, Natalie, typical of the Oudonovs, as his father would say, for the Oudonovs had always passed as eccentrics.

When he was born in their house at Archangel, where there had been eight servants, his father, who owned an important fishing fleet, had just left as an administrative officer for the army, and was somewhere behind the front line.

In order to be nearer to him his mother – a regular carrier-pigeon, as his father kept saying – had left with all her family in the train for Moscow and they had descended on Aunt Zina.

Her real name was Zinaida Oudonova, but he had always heard her called Aunt Zina.

She lived, according to his parents, in a house so big that you could lose yourself in the corridors, and she was very rich. It was in her house that Jonas fell ill at the age of six months. He had contracted an infectious form of pneumonia which he did not seem to be able to throw off, and the doctors had recommended the gentler climate of the South.

They had some friends in the Crimea, at Yalta, the Shepilovs, and without a word of warning, his mother had decided one morning to go to them with the baby.

'I leave the girls in your care, Zina,' she had said to the aunt. 'We shall be back in a few weeks, as soon as we've got the colour back into this lad's cheeks.'

It was not easy, in the middle of a war, to travel across Russia, but nothing was impossible for an Oudonov. Fortunately her mother had found the Shepilovs at Yalta. She had lingered, as was to be expected with her, and it was there that the Revolution had taken her by surprise.

There was no further news of the father. The daughters were still with Zina in Moscow, and Natalie talked about leaving the baby at Yalta to go and fetch them.

The Shepilovs had dissuaded her. Shepilov was a pessimist. The exodus was starting. Lenin and Trotsky were taking over power. The Wrangel army was being formed.

Why not go to Constantinople to let the storm pass, and return in a few months?

The Shepilovs had taken his mother and they had become part of the Russian colony which invaded the hotels of Turkey, some of them with money, others in search of any sort of employment to keep themselves alive.

The Shepilovs had managed to bring out some gold and jewellery. Natalie had a few diamonds with her.

Why had they gone on to Paris from Constantinople? And how, from Paris, had they finished up in a little town in the Berry?

It was not altogether a mystery. Shepilov, before the war, used to entertain lavishly on his estates in the Ukraine and thus he had entertained a certain number of French people, in particular, for several weeks at a time, the Comte de Coubert whose château and farms were some eight miles from Louvant.

They had met after the exodus, which they still thought of as purely temporary, and Coubert had suggested to Shepilov that he should install himself in his château. Natalie had followed, and with her Jonas, who had still no comprehensive grasp of the world across which he was being dragged in this way.

During this time Constantin Milk, who had been taken prisoner by the Germans, had been released at Aix-la-Chapelle following the armistice. He was given neither provisions nor money, nor any means of transport, and there was no question of returning under these circumstances to the distant soil of Russia.

Stage by stage, begging his way with others like himself, Milk had reached Paris and one day the Comte de Coubert had seen his name in a list of Russian prisoners recently arrived.

Nothing was known of Aunt Zina, or of the girls, who probably had not had time to cross the frontier.

Constantin Milk wore thick spectacles, as his son was soon to do, and, being short in the leg, had the build of a Siberian bear. He had quickly tired of the life of inaction in the château and, one evening, had announced that he had bought a fish-mongery in the town with Natalie's jewels.

'It may be a little hard for an Oudonov,' he had said with his enigmatic smile, 'but she'll jolly well have to get down to it.'

From his door Jonas could see the shop '*À la Marée*', with its two white marble counters and its big copper scales. He had lived for years on the first floor, in the room with the sky-light now occupied by Chenu's daughter.

Until the time he went to school he had spoken hardly anything but Russian and then had almost completely forgotten it.

Russia was for him a mysterious and bloody country where his five sisters, including Doussia, had very probably been massacred with Aunt Zina, like the Imperial family.

His father, like the Oudonovs whom he used to taunt, had also been a man of sudden decisions, or at any rate, if they matured slowly he never mentioned them to anyone.

In 1930, when Jonas was fourteen years old and going to the local *lycée*, Constantin Milk had announced that he was leaving for Moscow. As Natalie insisted that they should all go together, he had looked at his son and declared:

'*Better make sure that at least one of us is left!*'

Nobody knew what fate was in store for him out there. He had promised to send news somehow or other, but at the end of a year they had still heard nothing.

The Shepilovs had set up house in Paris where they had opened a bookshop in the rue Jacob, and Natalie had written to ask them whether they would look after Jonas, whom she had sent to a *lycée* in Paris, while she in her turn would undertake the journey to Russia.

That was how he came to enter Condorcet.

In the meantime another war had broken out, in which his eyesight had prevented him from taking part, whole populations had been disturbed once more, and there had been new exoduses, new waves of refugees.

Jonas had applied to all the authorities imaginable, Russian as well as French, without obtaining any news of his family.

Could he hope that his father, at eighty-two years old, and his mother, at seventy-six, were still alive?

What had happened to Aunt Zina, in whose house people

lost themselves, and his sisters, whose faces were unknown to him?

Did Doussia even know that she had a brother somewhere in the world.

All around him the walls were covered with old books. In his little room was a large stove which he kept roaring hot in winter as a luxury, and today he would have sworn that the smell of herrings still hung in the air in the kitchen.

The huge roof of the market was streaked with sunlight opposite his window and all around there were shops hardly larger than his own, except on the side of the rue de Bourges where St Cecilia's Church stood.

He could put a name to every face, recognize everyone's voice, and, when people saw him in his doorway or when he went into Le Bouc's, they used to call out:

'Hullo, Monsieur Jonas!'

It was a world in which he had shut himself up, and Gina had walked in one fine day with a sway of her hips, bringing a warm smell of armpits with her into this world of his.

She had just walked out again, and he was overcome with a fit of giddiness.

Chapter Four

It was not that day that the complications were to begin, but he still had the feeling of a person who is incubating an illness.

In the afternoon, fortunately, the customers were fairly numerous in the shop and he received, among others, a visit from Monsieur Legendre, a retired railway guard, who used to read a book a day, sometimes two, changed them by the half-dozen and always sat down in a chair for a chat. He used to smoke a meerschaum pipe which made a spluttering noise each time he sucked at it, and as he had a habit of pressing down the burning tobacco, the entire top joint of his index finger was a golden brown colour.

He was neither a widower nor a bachelor. His wife, small and thin, used to shop at the market, a black hat on her head, three times a week, and stop in front of all the stalls, disputing the price before buying a bunch of leeks.

Monsieur Legendre stayed for nearly an hour. The door was open. In the shadow of the covered market the cement, after being washed down, was drying slowly, leaving damp patches and, as it was Thursday, a crowd of children had taken possession of it and this time were playing at cowboys.

Two or three customers had interrupted the ex-railwayman's discourse and he waited, quite used to it, for the bookseller to finish serving them before carrying on the conversation at the exact point where he had left off.

'As I was saying . . .'

At seven o'clock, Jonas hesitated whether to lock up and go and have dinner at Pepito's as it seemed to him he ought to do, but finally he hadn't the heart. Instead he decided to walk across the Square and buy some eggs at Coutelle's, the dairy, where, as he expected, Madame Coutelle asked him:

'Isn't Gina there?'

It was without conviction, this time, that he replied:

'She's gone to Bourges.'

He made himself an omelette. It was good for him to keep himself occupied. His movements were meticulous. Just before pouring the whipped-up eggs into the pan he yielded once more to gluttony, as he had done at midday with the apple tart, and went into the yard to pick a few chives which were growing in a box.

Oughtn't he to have been indifferent to what he ate, seeing that Gina had gone? He arranged the butter, bread and coffee on the table, unfolded his napkin and ate his meal slowly, to all appearances thinking of nothing.

He had read in some book or other, probably war memoirs, that a certain time nearly always elapses before the most seriously wounded feel any pain, that sometimes they do not even realize at once that they have been hit.

In his case it was a little different. He felt no violent pain, nor despair. It was more that a void had been created inside him. He was no longer in a state of equilibrium. The kitchen, which had not changed, seemed to him not so much strange as lifeless, without any definite shape, as if he had been looking at it without his glasses.

He did not weep, did not sigh, that evening, any more than the day before. After eating a banana which had been bought by Gina, he did the washing-up, swept out the kitchen, then went over to the doorway to watch the sun setting.

He did not stay where he was because the Chaignes, the grocers from next door, had brought their chairs out on to the pavement and were chatting in low voices with the butcher, who had come to keep them company.

If he no longer had his valuable stamps at least he still had his collection of Russian ones, for this, which was purely of sentimental value, he had stuck into an album rather in the way that in other houses family portraits are pasted in.

Yet he did not feel himself to be particularly Russian – witness the fact that he only felt at home in the Vieux-Marché.

The shopkeepers had been friendly when the Milks had set themselves up there, and, although to start with Milk's father did not speak one word of French, he had soon made great headway. It sometimes provoked his great laugh, devoid of bitterness, to be selling fish by the pound when, a few years earlier, he owned the most important fishing fleet in Archangel, and his boats went as far as Spitzbergen and Novaya Zembla. A little while before the war he had even equipped his ships as whalers, and it was perhaps a sort of sense of humour all his own that prompted him to call his son Jonas.

Natalie was slower to adapt herself to their new life and her husband used to tease her in Russian in front of the customers, who did not understand a word.

'Come on, Ignatievna Oudonova, dip your pretty little hands into that tub and serve this fat lady with half a dozen whiting.'

Jonas knew practically nothing about the Oudonovs, his mother's family, except that they were merchants who provisioned boats. While Constantin Milk, whose grandfather was a shipowner before him, had kept some of his rough plebeian habits, the Oudonovs liked good manners and mixed in high society.

When he was in a good mood, Milk did not call his wife Natalie, but Ignatievna Oudonova, or simply Oudonova, and she would pout as if it were a reproach.

Her chief despair was that there were no synagogues in the town, for the Milks, like the Oudonovs, were Jews. There were other Jews in the district, especially among the second-hand shops and small stores in the rue Haute, but because the Milks were red-haired, with fair skin and blue eyes, the local people did not seem to be aware of their race.

To the world at large they were Russians, and in a sense it was true.

At school, at first, when he had hardly been able to speak French and often used comical expressions, Jonas had been the butt of many gibes, but it had not lasted long.

'They are very nice,' he would say to his parents when they asked him how his schoolmates treated him.

It was perfectly true. Everyone was nice to them. After his father's departure, nobody went into the shop without asking Natalie:

'Still no news?'

Jonas was rather proud at heart that his mother had abandoned him to go and join her husband. It had upset him more to leave the Old Market to go to Condorcet, and above all to meet the Shepilovs again.

Serge Sergeevitch Shepilov was an intellectual, and it could be seen in the attitudes he struck, in his way of speaking, of looking at the person he was talking to with a certain air of condescension. After eleven years of living in France he still regarded himself as an exile and went to all the White Russian meetings, worked for their newspaper and their reviews.

When Jonas used to go and see them on holidays, in the bookshop in the rue Jacob, at the back of which they lived in a minute studio, Shepilov liked to address him in Russian then, stopping short, would remark bitterly:

'Ah, but then you've forgotten the language of your country!'

Shepilov was still alive. So, too, was his wife, Nina Ignatievna. Both old now, they had eventually installed themselves in Nice where the odd article which Shepilov sold to a newspaper from time to time enabled them to vegetate. Around the

samovar they spent their declining years in the cult of the past
and the denigration of the present.

'If your father hasn't been shot or sent to Siberia, then it's
because he's rallied to the Party cause, in which case I prefer
never to see him again.'

Jonas hated nobody, not even the Bolsheviks, whose rise had
scattered his family. If he ever thought of Doussia, it was less
as a real person than as a sort of fairy. In his imagination
Doussia resembled nobody he knew; she had become the
symbol of fragile, tender femininity which brought tears to his
eyes every time he thought of it.

So as not to be left with nothing to do for the whole evening,
he turned over the pages of Russian stamps, and in the little
room where he had turned on the light, the history of his
country unfolded itself before his eyes.

This collection, almost complete, had taken him a long time
to build up, and it had required a great deal of patience, letters
and exchanges with hundreds of philatelists, even though the
entire album was worth less commercially than four or five of
the stamps Gina had taken away.

The first stamp, which was also the first issued in Russia,
dating from 1857, depicted an eagle in relief, and although Jonas
possessed the ten and twenty kopeks, he had never managed to
get hold of the thirty kopeks.

For years, the same symbol had been used with minor
variations until the tercentenary in 1905, which the school
friend from Condorcet had shown him.

Then with the 1914 war there came the charity stamps with
the portrait of Murometz and the Cossack of the Don. He
particularly liked, for its style and engraving, a St George
and the Dragon which, however, was only catalogued at forty
francs.

He thought to himself as he fondled them:

'When this stamp was issued my father was twenty years

old . . . He was twenty-five . . . He was meeting my mother . . . That one dates from Alyosha's birth . . .'

In 1917 it was the Phrygian cap of the Democratic Republic, with the two crossed sabres, then the stamps of Kerensky, on which a powerful hand was breaking a chain.

1921, 1922 saw the advent of illustrations with harder, coarser lines, and from 1923 onwards the commemorations started once again, no longer of the Romanovs, but of the fourth anniversary of the October Revolution, the fifth anniversary of the Soviet Republic.

Some more charity stamps at the time of the famine, then, with the USSR pictures of workers, ploughmen, soldiers, the portrait of Lenin, in red and black for the first time in 1924.

He did not soften or feel touched with nostalgia. It was more curiosity which had impelled him to assemble this collection of pictures of a far-off world and place them side by side.

A Samoyed village, or a group of Tajiks beside a cornfield, plunged him into the same dreamland as a child with a book of holy pictures.

The idea of going back there had never occurred to him, and it was not due to fear of the fate which might await him, nor, as with Shepilov, hatred for the Party.

From the moment he had come of age, on the contrary, two years before the war, he had renounced his 'Nansen' passport and become a naturalized Frenchman.

France itself was too big for him. After school he had worked for several months in a bookshop in the Boulevard Saint-Michel and the Shepilovs had been unable to believe their ears when he had told them that he preferred to return to the Berry.

He had gone back alone, had taken a furnished room with old Mademoiselle Buttereau, who had died during the war, and had gone to work as a clerk in Duret's bookshop, in the rue de Bourges.

It was still in existence. Old Duret had retired, almost gaga, but the two sons continued the business. It was the chief newsagent-bookshop in town and one of its windows was devoted to devotional objects.

He had not yet taken to eating at Pepito's at that time, because it was too expensive. When the bookseller's shop, where he now lived, had become vacant, he had moved in there as if the rue de Bourges, only a stone's throw away, had been too far.

He was back once again in the heart of the Old Market of his childhood and everyone had recognized him.

Gina's departure had suddenly destroyed this equilibrium, acquired by perseverance, with the same brutality as the Revolution, earlier on, had scattered his own family.

He did not peruse the album to the end. He made himself a cup of coffee, went and removed the handle from the door, turned the key in the lock, shot the bolt, and a little while later went up to his room.

It was, as always when there was no market, a quiet night, without any noise except for the occasional distant motor horn, and the even more distant rumble of a goods train.

Alone in his bed, without the spectacles which made him look like a man, he huddled up like a frightened child and finally went to sleep, with a sad twist to his lips, one hand in the place where Gina ought to have been.

When the sun woke him, coming into his room, the air was still as calm as ever and the bells of St Cecilia's were sounding out the first Mass. All of a sudden he felt the void of his loneliness again, and he almost dressed without washing as sometimes happened before Gina's day. But he was intent at all costs on following the same routine as every other day, so that he even hesitated when he was being served his croissants at the baker's opposite.

'Only three,' he finally murmured regretfully.

'Isn't Gina there?'

These people didn't know yet. True, they were almost new to the Square, where they had bought the business only five years before.

'No. She's not there.'

He was surprised not to be pressed, that the news was received with indifference.

It was half past seven. He hadn't closed the door to go across the Square. He never did. When he came back he had a shock, for a man rose before him and as he was walking with his eyes cast down, plunged in thought, he had not recognized him immediately.

'Where is my sister?' Frédo's hard voice was demanding.

He stood in the middle of the shop, in a leather jerkin, his black hair still damp, showing the track of his comb.

Since the day before, Jonas had been expecting something to happen, but he was taken by surprise, and still holding his croissants in their brown tissue paper wrappings, he stammered:

'She hasn't come back.'

Frédo was as big as, and broader in the shoulders than, his father, and when he became angry, his nostrils would palpitate, alternately dilating and closing together.

'Where has she gone?' he went on, without taking his suspicious gaze off Jonas.

'I . . . but . . . to Bourges.'

He added, and perhaps it was a mistake, especially addressed to Frédo:

'At any rate she said she was going to Bourges.'

'When did she say that?'

'Yesterday morning.'

'What time?'

'I don't remember. Before the bus left.'

'Did she take the 7.10 bus yesterday morning?'

'She must have done.'

Why was he trembling in front of a mere boy of nineteen, who was taking liberties in demanding an explanation from him? He wasn't the only one in the neighbourhood to be afraid of Frédo. Since his earliest childhood the Palestri boy had had a sullen character, some even said sinister.

True, he didn't seem to like anybody, except his sister. With his father, when the latter had had too much to drink, he behaved intolerably and the neighbours had overheard some highly unsavoury rows. It was said that once Frédo had hit Palestri, and that his mother had gone for him, locked him up in his room like a ten-year-old.

He had climbed out through the window over the roofs, had stayed away for a week, during which time he had looked in vain for work at Montluçon.

He had not passed his certificate at school and had refused to learn any proper trade. He had worked with a few shop-keepers as errand-boy, delivery-man, later as a salesman. Nowhere had he remained for more than a few months or a few weeks.

He was not lazy. As one of his ex-employers said:

'That lad rebels against any form of discipline. He wants to be a general before being a plain soldier.'

As much as Jonas liked the Old Market, Frédo appeared to hate it, just as he despised and hated, in the mass, its inhabitants, as, no doubt, he would have hated anywhere he had happened to be.

Angèle alone liked to treat him as if he were still a child, but it was by no means certain that she wasn't a little afraid as well. When he was fifteen she had found a long clasp-knife in his pocket, which he spent hours fondly sharpening. She had taken it away from him. He had said, unconcerned:

'I'll buy another.'

'I forbid you to do any such thing!'

'By what right?'

'Because I'm your mother!'

'As if you'd become it on purpose! I bet my father was drunk!'

He didn't drink himself, didn't go dancing, used to frequent a small bar in the Italian quarter, in the shady part of the rue Haute where Poles and Arabs mixed and where there were always to be seen groups of men holding disquieting conferences in the back of the room. The place was called the Luxor Bar. Following Marcel's hold-up the police had taken an interest in it, for Marcel, before Frédo, had been a regular customer.

All they had found had been a retired boxer on probation, whose papers were not in order. Ever since they had nevertheless kept their eye on the Luxor Bar.

Jonas was not afraid in the real sense of the word. Even if Frédo had hit him in a moment of fury, it would not have mattered to him. He was not brave, but he knew that physical pain does not last indefinitely.

It was Gina whom he felt he was defending at this moment, and he had the impression that he was making a mess of it. He could have sworn that his face had reddened to the roots of his hair.

'Did she say she would not be coming back to sleep?'

'I . . .'

He thought very rapidly. Once already when the question of Bourges had arisen, he had spoken without thinking. This time he must take care.

'I don't remember.'

The young man sneered derisively.

'So you can't remember whether you were to expect her or not?'

'She didn't know herself.'

'Well then, did she take her travelling-case?'

Think fast, all the time, and not get caught out, not contradict himself. He couldn't help glancing at the staircase.

'I don't think so.'

'She didn't take it,' Frédo stated.

His voice grew hard, became accusing.

'Her case is in the cupboard, and her coat.'

He was waiting for an explanation. What could Jonas reply? Was this the moment to admit the truth? Was it to Gina's brother that he was to make his confession?

He stiffened, managed to say curtly:

'Possibly.'

'She didn't take the bus to Bourges.'

He feigned astonishment.

'I had a friend in the bus and he didn't see her.'

'Perhaps she took the train.'

'To go to see La Loute?'

'I imagine so.'

'Gina didn't go to see La Loute either. I rang her up this morning before coming here.'

Jonas did not know that La Loute had a telephone, or that Frédo was on speaking terms with her. If he knew her number perhaps he had already been to call on her there himself?

'Where is my sister?'

'I don't know.'

'When did she leave?'

'Yesterday morning.'

He almost added:

'I swear!'

He almost believed it, by sheer force of repetition. What difference did it make if Gina had left on Wednesday evening or Thursday morning?

'Nobody saw her.'

'People are so used to seeing her passing that no one takes any notice now.'

Frédo, who was a whole head taller than he was, seemed to be hesitating whether to seize him by the shoulders and shake him, and Jonas, resigned, didn't move. His eyes didn't flinch until the moment that his visitor turned away to walk over to the door, without touching him.

'We'll soon see . . .' Frédo growled heavily.

Never had a morning been so bright and so calm. The Square had scarcely come to life and the sound of the grocer lowering his orange blind could be heard, with the handle squeaking out in the silence.

Standing in the doorway, Frédo was a huge and menacing shadow.

As he turned his back, he opened his mouth, no doubt for some insult, thought better of it, walked across the pavement, and started up his motor-bike.

Jonas was still standing motionless in the middle of the shop, forgetting his croissants, forgetting that it was breakfast time. He was trying to understand. Already the day before he had had a premonition of danger hanging over him, and now he had just been threatened under his own roof.

What for? Why?

He had done nothing except to take a wife into his house, whom Angèle had given to him, and for two years he had done his best to give her peace.

'*She's gone to Bourges . . .*'

He had said it without thinking, to stave off questions, and now it was bringing new ones in its wake. While he was at the baker's, Frédo had not only come into his house, but had gone upstairs, opened the cupboard, searched the wardrobe, since he knew that his sister had not taken her suitcase or coat.

Was it possible that *they* might be thinking what had suddenly come into his mind?

From red, he turned suddenly pale, so absurd and terrible was the notion. Did they really believe it? Had it really occurred to anybody, whether Frédo or not, that he had disposed of Gina?

Didn't they all know, everybody in the Old Market, and in

the town as well, that it was not his wife's first escapade, that she had had them before marrying him, when she still lived with her parents, and that this was the reason they had given her to him?

He had no illusions about that. Nobody else would have married her. And Gina did not have the calm, the sangfroid of La Loute, who more or less got away with it in Bourges.

She was a female who could not control herself, that they all knew, including her father.

Why in Heaven's name would he have . . . ?

Even in his mind he hesitated to formulate the word, or to think of it. But wasn't it better to face the reality?

Why would he have killed her?

It was that, he was sure, that Frédo suspected. And perhaps, the day before, the same idea had already come, in a vaguer form, in Palestri's mind.

Otherwise why were they pestering him so?

If he was jealous, if he suffered every time Gina went off after a man, every time he detected an alien smell about her, he had never let anybody see it, not even her. He had never reproached her. On the contrary! When she returned, he was more gentle than ever, to help her forget, to prevent her from feeling uncomfortable in his presence.

He needed her as well. He wanted to keep her. He did not consider that he had the right to shut her up, as Angèle had once shut up her son.

Were they really thinking that?

He was on the point of running round to the Palestris' at once to tell Angèle the truth, but he realized that he was too late. He would no longer be believed. He had too often repeated that she had gone to Bourges, had given too many details.

Perhaps she would come back, in spite of everything? The fact that she had not taken her coat perplexed him. For if she had hidden in some part of the town why should she have taken the stamps, which she would not have been able to sell?

Mechanically he had gone into the kitchen, and once again, with mechanical gestures, he was making coffee, sitting down to drink it and eat his croissants. The Chaignes's lime tree was full of birds and he opened the door into the yard to throw them crumbs as usual.

If only it had been possible for him to question the clerk at the station, he would know, but it was too late for that, too.

Was somebody waiting for Gina with a car? That would have explained her going off without her coat. He could still present himself to the police and tell them everything, ask them to make inquiries for him. Who could tell? Tomorrow they would very likely reprimand him for not having done so, and see in that a proof against him!

Still unthinking, he went up to the bedroom where the door of the cupboard and the two doors of the wardrobe stood wide open. There was even a pair of his trousers on the floor. He put them back in their place, made the bed, cleaned out the bathroom and changed his dirty towel. It was laundry day and he thought about getting the dirty washing ready, as Gina was not there to do it. In the basket, which he emptied, there were some petticoats and brassières; he had begun to list the various items, when he was interrupted by steps downstairs.

It was Madame Lallemand, the mother of the little invalid girl who had been to Bourges the day before. She had come in to change some books for her daughter.

'What did the doctor say?' he remembered to ask.

'It seems there's a specialist in Vienna who might be able to cure her. It isn't certain and there'd be the business of the journey, and staying there several months in a foreign country without being able to speak the language. It all costs a lot of money. My daughter says she would rather stay as she is, but all the same I'm going to write to her uncle, who has a good business in Paris and may be able to help us.'

While he was choosing the books, the woman seemed to notice the silence in the house where, at that time, Gina would normally have been heard moving about.

'Isn't your wife in?'

He confined himself to a shake of the head.

'Yesterday somebody asked my daughter if she'd been with her on the bus.'

'You don't know who?'

'I didn't ask. I have so little time for other people, you see . . .'

He did not react. From now on he was prepared for everything. His principal feeling was not even fear, but disappointment and yet he had never expected anything from other people, had been content to live in his own corner, as humbly as possible.

'I think she would enjoy these two.'

'There's nothing about sick people in them?'

'No. I've read them.'

It was true that he sometimes read novels meant for young girls and actually enjoyed them. On these occasions he would think of Doussia, whom he would picture as each of the heroines in turn.

After that the gas bill was brought and he opened the till, paid, intended to go upstairs to finish off the laundry, when a young man brought in some school books to sell to him. Jonas was sure that he would come in a week or two to buy them back, that he was selling them only because he was short of pocket money. But as other people's affairs were no concern of his, he made an offer.

'Is that all?'

He was still a businessman.

'If they were not in such bad condition . . .'

There were three shelves of them, all school books, and it was these that brought in the most money, because the editions seldom changed, and the same books would pass through his hands a great many times in a few years. There were some he recognized, by a stain on the cover, for example, before he so much as touched them.

In the end he was able to go upstairs, finish off his list, tie up the dirty washing in a pillow case which he hid under the counter to await the arrival of the laundry man. It did not seem odd to him to send Gina's washing to the laundry. In his mind she was still, always would be, part of the household.

At ten o'clock he went over to Le Bouc's bar, where there was only a lorry driver whom he didn't know. He heard the usual:

' 'Morning, Monsieur Jonas.'

And he gave the ritual response:

' 'Morning, Fernand. An espresso coffee, please.'

'There you are.'

He picked up his two bits of sugar and began to unwrap them. The driver held his glass of white wine in his hand and said nothing, all the time keeping an eye on his lorry through the window. Contrary to his usual habit, Le Bouc worked the percolator in silence, and Jonas thought he seemed uncomfortable.

He had been expecting one question, and as it did not come, he volunteered:

'Gina hasn't come back.'

Fernand murmured, placing the steaming cup on the counter:

'So they tell me.'

So they had been talking about it here too. Not Frédo, surely, who did not frequent the bars of the Vieux-Marché. Was it Louis? But how would Louis have known, since his son, when he left, had gone off in the direction of the town?

They had certainly questioned the young cripple as she stepped out of the bus!

He couldn't understand it any longer. There was something

entirely beyond him in this undercurrent of distrust. The time that Gina had been away for three days there had been no talk and, at most, a few people had given her a lewd glance.

Only the butcher had commented:

'How's your wife?'

He had replied:

'Very well, thank you.'

And Ancel had exclaimed, with a conspiratorial look at the assembled company:

'Heavens above!'

Why were they making a tragedy out of what had amused them only six months earlier? If he had been alone with Le Bouc, he would have been tempted to ask him. He probably would not have done so when all was said and done, from pure shame, but he would have felt like it.

And why did he need to explain himself, as though he felt guilty? Even now, he could not prevent himself from saying, with ill-affected indifference:

'She must have been held up.'

Le Bouc contented himself with a sigh, and avoided his gaze:

'No doubt.'

What had he done to them? Yesterday morning, when Gina had already departed, he still felt he was on good terms with them.

They were letting him drop all of a sudden, without a word of explanation, without letting him show his defence.

He had done nothing, nothing!

Was he going to be forced to shout it out aloud to them?

He was so upset that he inquired, as if he had not always known, the price of his coffee:

'How much is that?'

'The usual: thirty francs.'

They must be talking about him all over the Square. There were rumours of which he knew nothing. Somewhere there must have been a misunderstanding which a few words would suffice to clear up.

'I'm beginning to be anxious,' he went on, with a forced smile.

The observation fell flat. Le Bouc stood before him like a wall.

Jonas was making a mistake. He was talking too much. He gave the impression of defending himself before he had been accused. And nobody would ever dare to accuse him of getting rid of Gina.

Frédo, perhaps. But everyone knew him to be hot-headed.

Once again he was not guilty of anything. He had nothing to hide. If he had mentioned Bourges, it was out of tact on Gina's behalf. He had not opened the strong-box then, and he envisaged an affair lasting a night or a couple of days. Would he have done better to reply to the people asking him for news of his wife: 'She's in bed with some man or other'?

They must believe him if he affirmed that it was not from vanity or self-respect that he had spoken about Bourges. If he had been vain, he would not have married Gina, whom nobody wanted, and it had given rise to enough laughter in the neighbourhood to see her married in white. Angèle herself had tried to oppose it.

'All my friends were married in white,' Gina had answered.

'Your friends aren't you.'

'I don't know one who was a virgin when she married, if that's what you mean, and you weren't one either when you married Papa.'

What she said of her friends and her mother was probably quite true. Anyhow, Angèle had made no reply. Only the others had not advertised themselves as much as she had.

If he had been ridiculous, as well, in his get-up, he had none the less looked around him proudly as he left the church with her arm in his.

He was not vain. He was not ashamed of what she was.

And yet he had just tried to lie to himself, by convincing himself that it was for her sake, and not for his own, that he had invented the trip to Bourges.

From what would he have wanted to shield her, since she had never made any secret of her escapades? As for the others, they must have enjoyed seeing her deceive him and been grateful to him for the fun they derived from it.

All the same he had answered:

'*She's gone to Bourges.*'

After that he had stuck to it doggedly.

As he made for his shop, where a stranger was browsing among the books in the cases outside, he was trying to find the answer, or rather to accept, since it gave him no satisfaction to do so.

If he had felt the need to protect Gina, wasn't it ultimately because he felt guilty towards her?

He didn't want to think about it any more. It was quite enough to have gone as far as he had. If he went on in this vein God knows where he would end in his discovery of things better left undiscovered.

Besides, nobody knew about all that. It was not what they were going to accuse him of. He had not killed her. He had not got rid of her. He was not guilty in their sense of the word.

Why, from that moment on, did they all, even Le Bouc, whom he liked best of the lot, to whose bar he went more as a friend than for love of coffee, why did they all look on him with suspicion?

'How much is this?' the customer asked him, holding out a book on underwater fishing.

'The price is marked on the back. A hundred and twenty francs.'

'A hundred francs,' the other suggested.

He repeated:

'A hundred and twenty.'

He must have spoken in an unusual tone of voice, for the man hastily dug into his pocket for the money, looking at him in astonishment.

Chapter Five

They left him alone until the Monday, too much alone in fact, for he was beginning to believe they were creating a vacuum around him. Perhaps he was becoming too susceptible and prone to read non-existent motives into people's actions?

After badgering him for two whole days for news of Gina with as much insistence as if they were dunning him, they no longer mentioned it to him, and he was beginning to suspect them, Le Bouc, Ancel, and the others, of deliberately avoiding all reference to his wife.

Why did they abruptly cease taking any interest in her? And if they knew where she was, what reason had they for keeping it from him?

He was on the watch for the slightest nuance. For example, when he had lunched at Pepito's on the Friday, the Widower had then distinctly batted his eyelids at him just as he used to in the old days, whereas yesterday they had scarcely flickered. Was the chief clerk under the impression that Jonas had returned for good and would be once again having his meals opposite him every day?

Pepito was not surprised to see him back, but he hadn't asked for news of Gina.

'There is creamed cod today,' he had announced, knowing that Jonas liked it.

It could not have been said that his manner was exactly cold, but he was certainly more reserved than usual.

'Will you be dining here this evening?' he had asked as Jonas rose to leave.

'I don't think so.'

Logically, Pepito ought to have remarked:

'Is Gina coming back this afternoon?'

For Pepito did not know the reason why Jonas, although he was alone, preferred to have dinner at home. In actual fact it was in order not to resume, all at once, his bachelor's existence, in order not to sever all the links with the other life he had known, and also because getting his meal and washing up afterwards kept him occupied.

The afternoon had been gloomy. The sultry air had penetrated through the open doorway. Jonas had settled down to sorting and marking one of the batches of books he brought down from the stock in the loft, where there were all kinds, the majority of them school prizes, which still bore in faded ink the names of their winners, long since deceased.

There had been few customers. Louis had passed by on his three-wheeler, slowing up, but had not stopped until reaching Fernand's bar.

At four o'clock, by which time he had departed, Jonas had gone for his coffee and Le Bouc had shown the same reserve as he had in the morning. Next he had repaired to Ancel's to buy a cutlet for his dinner. Ancel was not there. His assistant served him and Madame Ancel appeared from the back of the shop to take the money without asking any questions.

He had dinner, tidied up, continued working fairly late on his inventory of the attic stock, which stood in a large pile in a corner, and patching the torn volumes with adhesive paper.

He worked in the shop where there was a light, but he had removed the door handle. The rest of the house was in darkness. Somebody walked past and back again around nine o'clock; he only half saw the figure in the darkness and he would have sworn it was Angèle.

They were spying on him. Without asking him anything, they were coming to see if Gina was back.

He went to bed at ten o'clock, fell asleep, and soon the sounds of an eve-of-market night began. Saturday's market was the most important one and, at certain hours of the day, the cars had to mount the pavement to find a parking space. It was hotter than the day before. The sun, a light yellow hue, no longer had the same airiness, and towards eleven o'clock it was as if a storm were going to break, and the market women could be seen peering anxiously at the sky. It broke somewhere in the country, for there was a rumbling in the distance, after which the clouds became luminous once more and finally disappeared, leaving nothing but an untrammelled blue.

He ate at Pepito's again and the Widower was there with his dog. It was Jonas who this time, as if seeking some sort of sympathy, of support, however, vague, was the first to flutter his eyelids, and Monsieur Métras returned the salute with a face devoid of expression.

Pepito's was closed on Sundays and Jonas made the round of the shops to buy his provisions, carrying Gina's straw shopping basket. He did not buy his vegetables at Angèle's but at a shop in the rue Haute. At the butcher's, Ancel served him in person this time, without the remotest suggestion of a friendly jest. He also had to buy some bread, some coffee, and some more salt, which had run out, and, for Sunday evening, he took home some spaghetti. It was a tradition from Gina's day, because it was quick to make.

The floor of the Old Market was washed down with hoses, a few cars came and parked in it and then in the evening, like the day before, he spent his time patching up books and marking the prices in pencil on the back. He had looked through the newspaper. He was not expecting to find news of his wife, nor indeed hoping for it, for that would have meant bad news, but he was nevertheless disappointed.

It was the fourth night that he had slept alone, and as he had gone to bed early, he heard some of the neighbours returning from the cinema; the following morning, before he got up, he heard others, women for the most part, making for St Cecilia's Church.

Ever since he had married Gina, he had accompanied her to Mass on Sundays, always the ten o'clock High Mass, and for this occasion she dressed up in her best clothes, in summer wore a blue suit with a hat and white gloves.

When the question of the wedding had arisen, he had realized that for the Palestri family it would have to take place in church.

Up till then he had never been inside it except for a few funerals, had never observed the rites of any religion, except, up to his mother's departure, the Jewish ones.

He had not said he was a Jew, nor hidden the fact. Immediately after the decision had been taken, he had gone to find the parish priest of St Cecilia's, Abbé Grimault, and had asked to be baptized.

For a period of three weeks he had taken catechism lessons at the priest's house almost every evening, in a little parlour with a round table covered with a crimson velvet cloth with tassels. The air was pervaded with a smell, at once stale and strong, which Jonas had never come across before, and which he was never to find again, anywhere else.

While he was reciting his lessons like a schoolboy, the Abbé Grimault, who was born on a farm in the Charolais, would puff at his cigar and gaze into space, which did not prevent him, however, from correcting his pupil the moment he went wrong.

Jonas had asked that he should not be treated too strictly and the priest had understood. Even so, a godfather and godmother had to be found. Justine, the Abbé's servant, and old Joseph, the sacristan, an engraver by trade, filled these rôles, and Jonas gave them each a handsome present. He gave another to the church. He had written to tell Shepilov that he was getting married, but had not dared mention the christening, nor the religious ceremony.

It had given him pleasure to become a Christian, not only because of the marriage, but because it brought him nearer to the inhabitants of the Old Market, nearly all of whom went to church. At first he stood a little stiffly and made his genu-flexions and signs of the cross out of time, but then he had picked up the habit and Gina and he kept to the same places every Sunday, at the end of a row.

He went to Mass that Sunday as on every other Sunday, and it was the first time he had gone alone. They seemed to be watching him as he went to his place, and to nudge one another as he passed.

He did not pray, because he had never really prayed, but he wanted to, and as he watched the dancing light of the candles and breathed the smell of the incense, he thought of Gina and also of his sister Doussia, though he never knew what she looked like.

After the service, groups formed outside the church and for a quarter of an hour the Square was full of life. The Sunday clothes lent a gay note, then, little by little, the pavements emptied and for the rest of the day there was virtually nobody to be seen there.

At noon Ancel, who worked on Sunday mornings, drew his blinds. All the other blinds in the Square were already lowered, except those of the bakery and cake shop which closed at half past twelve.

For Jonas and his wife, it was the day for the backyard. This meant that in good weather they would base themselves in the yard, as long as they were not going out. It was in fact almost impossible to stay in the shop in the summer with the door shut, because of the lack of air, and if the door was left open the

85

passers-by would think they were not observing their Sabbath rest.

Not only did they spend the afternoon in the courtyard but they lunched there as well, under the lime-tree branch which stretched over the Chaignes's garden wall and gave them some shade.

The whole length of the wall was covered by a vine, old and twisted, its leaves marked with rust, but it none the less produced each year a few bunches of acid grapes.

They had tried keeping a cat. They had had several. All of them, for some reason or other, had gone to seek a home elsewhere.

Gina didn't like dogs. Actually she didn't like any animals, and when they went for a walk in the country, she would eye the cows uneasily from a safe distance.

She didn't like the country either, nor taking walks. She had never wanted to learn to swim. She was only in her element when her extremely high heels came in contact with the hard smooth surface of a pavement, and she had in addition a horror of quiet streets like the one in which Clémence lived; she needed animation, noise, the many-coloured display of shop windows.

When they went to have a drink, she did not choose the spacious cafés of the Place de l'Hôtel de Ville, or the Place du Théâtre, but the bars with juke boxes.

He had bought her a wireless set and on Sundays she would take it out into the yard, using an extension to plug it into the kitchen.

She hardly ever sewed, was content to keep her clothes and linen more or less in disrepair, and her blouses were often missing a button, while a good half of her petticoats had holes in them.

She used to read, listening to the music and smoking cigarettes, and sometimes in the middle of the afternoon she would go up to her bedroom, remove her dress, and stretch out on top of the cover.

He read on this Sunday, too, in one of the two iron chairs which he had bought second-hand for use in the yard. He went back into the shop twice to change his book and in the end became interested in a work on the life of spiders. There was one in the corner, which he had known for a long time, and now and then he raised his eyes to observe it with renewed interest, like a man who has just made a discovery.

The post had brought him no news of Gina the day before or on Friday. He had been hoping, without believing it, that she would perhaps send him a word, and now he was beginning to realize that the idea was ridiculous.

From time to time, without interrupting his reading, his thoughts superimposed themselves on the printed text, without his losing the place. True they were not clear cut, consecutive thoughts. Various images came to his mind, such as that of Angèle, then, straightaway afterwards, for no reason, he pictured Gina lying naked on an iron bed, in a hotel bedroom.

Why an iron bed? And why, all round her, whitewashed walls, like those in the country?

It was unlikely that she had taken refuge in the country, which she detested. She was certainly not alone. Since Wednesday evening when she had left she must have bought herself some underclothes, unless she had been content to wash her petticoat and brassière at night and put them on again in the morning unironed.

Clémence, her husband and Poupou must have been with the Ancels, where the whole family used to gather and the youngest of the daughters, Martine, played the piano. They had a very large yard with, at the back, the shed Gina had talked about. She had not told him whether she had allowed the butcher to have her. Probably she had, but it was also probable that Ancel had not dared to go the whole way.

87

Twice during the afternoon he thought he heard the piano, the sound of which reached his backyard when the wind was in the right direction.

The Chaigne family had a car and were not at home on Sundays. Angèle used to sleep the entire afternoon while Louis, dressed in a navy-blue suit, went to play skittles and did not return until he had made a tour of the town's cafés.

How did a young man like Frédo spend his time? Jonas had no idea. He was the only one in the family not to go to Mass and he was not to be seen all day.

At five o'clock a few old women passed by on their way to Benediction and the bells rang out for a moment. Le Bouc's bar was closed. Jonas had made himself some coffee and, feeling slightly hungry, he nibbled a piece of cheese.

Nothing else happened. He had dined, after which, not having the heart to work, he had finished his book on spiders. It was only nine o'clock and he had gone for a stroll, closing the door behind him, had headed in the direction of the narrow canal where a lock-gate stood out black against the moonlit sky. Two narrow barges, of the Berry type, were moored to the quay and he could see rings forming around them on the surface of the water.

He passed Clémence's, in the rue des Deux-Ponts, and this time there was a light on the first floor. Did Clémence know something about Gina? Even if she did, she wouldn't tell him anything. He did not stop, as he was tempted to do, but passed quickly by, for the window was open and Reverdi, in shirt sleeves, was moving about the room talking.

The nearer he got to his home, the more the closed shutters in the streets, the deserted pavements, the silence, filled him with a sort of uneasiness, and he caught himself increasing his pace as if to flee from some indefinable menace.

Was it because others, like Gina, felt the same fear that they hurried into the garishly lighted bars, to seek the company of shouts and music?

He could see some of those bars in the distance, in the second part of the rue Haute, on the same side as the Luxor, and he could just make out the couples along the walls.

He slept badly, still with the feeling of a threat, which had pursued him even into his bedroom. He had removed his spectacles and switched off the light when a memory had jangled in his brain, not exactly a personal memory, for the passage of time had confused the fragments of what he had seen and heard with what he had subsequently been told.

He was not six years old when the drama had occurred, and since then there had been no further sensational events in the town until the Marcel hold-up.

He was born in 1916, so it had taken place in 1922, and he was just starting to go to school. It must have been November. The Maison Bleue was already in existence, so called because the outside was painted in sky-blue from top to bottom.

It had not changed since then. It stood surmounted by a very steep roof, at the corner of the rue des Prémontrés and the Square, just beside Ancel's butcher's shop, two houses from the fishmonger's where Jonas lived at the time.

The sign had not changed either. In letters of a darker blue than the façade was written: '*La Maison Bleue*'. Then, in smaller letters: '*Children's clothing. Baby garments a speciality.*'

The woman now known as the widow Lentin still had her husband at the time, a fair-haired man who wore long moustaches and who, since his wife ran the business, worked at odd jobs outside.

At certain periods, he could be seen sitting all day long on a chair in front of the house, and Jonas remembered a phrase he had heard frequently repeated:

'*Lentin's having one of his bouts.*'

Gustave Lentin had fought in the Tonkin campaign, a name which Jonas had heard for the first time when people were talking of him, and which to Jonas seemed a terrible word. He had caught the fevers there, as the people of the Vieux-Marché put it. For weeks he was like any other man, with a rather dark, at times stormy look in his eyes, and he would embark on some job or other. Then it would get around that he was in bed, 'covered with an icy sweat and trembling in his limbs, his teeth clenched like a dead man's'.

Jonas had not invented this description. He did not know where he had heard it, but it had remained engraved on his memory. Doctor Lourel, since dead, who had worn a beard, came to see him twice a day, striding rapidly, his worn leather bag in his hand, and Jonas, from the pavement opposite, used to glue his eyes to the windows, wondering if Lentin was dying.

A few days later he would reappear, emaciated, his eyes sad and empty, and his wife would help him out on to his chair beside the doorway, would move him during the day, as the sun followed its course.

The shop did not belong to Lentin but to his parents-in-law, the Arnauds, who lived in the house with the couple. Madame Arnaud remained in Jonas's mind as a woman almost entirely round, with white hair gathered in a bun at the back of her head and so sparse that the pink of her skull showed through it.

He could not remember her husband.

But he had seen the crowd, one morning, as he was about to leave for school. There was a wind blowing that day. It was a market day. An ambulance and two other black cars were standing in front of the Maison Bleue and the crowd was shoving so much that one might have thought it was a riot, if it had not been for the oppressive silence which reigned.

Although his mother had dragged him away and assured him afterwards that he could not have seen anything, he was convinced, to this day, that he had seen on a stretcher carried by two male nurses in white smocks, a man with his throat cut. A woman was screaming, he was sure, in the house, in the way that mad women scream.

'You imagine you actually saw what you heard told afterwards.'

It was possible, but it was difficult to admit that that image had not really appeared before his eyes as a child.

Lentin, it was afterwards learnt, suffered from the feeling of being a useless passenger in the house of his in-laws. Several times he was said to have let it be known that things would not go on as they were, and they had imagined suicide. They used to watch him. His wife sometimes followed in the street at a discreet distance.

That night he had not woken her up, even though he was racked with fever. She had been the first down, as usual, imagining him still sleeping and then, silently, a razor in his hand, he had gone into the bedroom of his father- and mother-in-law and had cut their throats one after the other as he had seen done by the Tonkinese soldiers, and as, out there, he had perhaps done himself.

Only old Madame Arnaud had had the time to cry out. Her daughter had rushed up the stairs, but when she reached the open door her husband had finished his work and, standing in the middle of the room and fixing her with a 'mad look', he had in turn severed his own carotid artery.

Madame Lentin was quite white now, diminutive, her hair as thin as her mother's, and she went on selling children's clothing and baby garments.

Why had Jonas thought of this drama just as he was dropping off to sleep? Because he had passed in front of the Maison Bleue a short while ago and had had a glimpse of a shadow behind the curtain?

It disturbed him. He forced himself to think of something else. As he was still not able to sleep after half an hour he got up to take a tablet of gardenal. In fact he took two, and the effect was almost immediate. Only towards four o'clock he awoke in the silence of the dawn and lay with his eyes open until it was time to get up.

He was stiff and uncomfortable. He almost decided against going to the baker for his croissants, as he was not hungry, but it was a form of discipline he had imposed on himself and he crossed the deserted Square, saw Angèle laying her baskets out on the pavement. Did she see him? Did she pretend not to see him?

'Three?' the baker's wife asked him from force of habit.

It annoyed him. He had the impression he was being spied on, and above all that the others knew things he did not. Ancel, without taking the cigarette from his lips, was unloading some sides of beef, which did not even cause him to stoop, and yet he must have been five or six years older than Jonas.

He ate, took out his boxes of books, decided to finish off the stock from the attic before going up to his room, and at half past nine he was still working, looking in a bibliography to see whether a dilapidated Maupassant which he had just found in the pile was a first edition.

Somebody came in and he did not immediately raise his eyes. He knew, by the silhouette, that it was a man, and the latter, without pressing him, was examining the books on a shelf.

When he finally looked up, Jonas recognized Police Inspector Basquin, to whom he had on many occasions sold books.

'Excuse me,' he stammered. 'I was busy with . . .'

'How are you, Monsieur Jonas?'

'All right. I'm all right.'

He could have sworn that Basquin had not come that morning to buy a book from him, more especially as he had one in his hand.

'And Gina?'

He reddened. It was unavoidable. The more he tried not to the more he reddened, and he felt his ears burning.

'I trust she's all right, too.'

Basquin was three or four years younger than he and had been born the far side of the canal, in a group of five or six houses surrounding the brickworks. He was fairly often to be seen at the market, and if ever one of the shopkeepers was robbed, it was nearly always he who took charge of it.

'Isn't she here?'

He hesitated, first said no, then, like a man plunging into the water, said all in one breath:

'She left on Wednesday evening telling me that she was going to look after the baby for Ancel's daughter, Clémence. Since then she hasn't come back and I've heard no news.'

It was a relief finally to let out the truth, to dispose once and for all of this fairy tale about the visit to Bourges, which was haunting him. Basquin looked a decent sort of fellow. Jonas had heard tell that he had five children, a very blonde wife with a sickly appearance, who in reality was more hardy than some women who appear outwardly strong.

In this way, often, in the Old Market, one learns the history of people one has never seen, by odds and ends of conversations picked up here and there. Jonas did not know Madame Basquin, who lived in a small new house on the edge of the town, but it was possible that he had seen her when she was doing her shopping, without realizing who she was.

The Inspector did not have a crafty look, as though he wanted to catch Jonas out. He was relaxed, familiar, as he stood by the counter, book in hand, like a customer talking about the rain or the fine weather.

'Did she take any luggage with her?'

'No. Her case is upstairs.'

'And her dresses, her clothes?'

'She was only wearing her red dress.'

'No coat?'

Didn't that prove that Basquin knew more than he wanted to show? Why, otherwise, would he have thought of the coat? Frédo had thought of it, certainly, but only after searching in the bedroom.

Did that mean that Frédo had warned the police?

'Her two coats are in the cupboard as well.'

'Had she any money on her?'

'If she had, it wasn't much.'

His heart was thumping against his constricted chest and he had difficulty in speaking naturally.

'You have no idea where she might have gone?'

'None, Monsieur Basquin. At half past twelve on Wednesday night, I was so worried that I went round to Clémence's.'

'What did she tell you?'

'I didn't go in. There wasn't any light. I thought that they were all in bed and I didn't want to disturb them. I hoped that Gina might have come back another way.'

'You didn't meet anyone?'

That was the question which frightened him most of all, for he realized that what he was being asked for was an alibi. He searched desperately in his memory, then confessed, abashed:

'No. I don't think so.'

A recollection occurred to him.

'I heard a couple talking in the rue de Bourges, but I didn't see them.'

'You didn't pass anyone, either going or coming back?'

'I don't remember. I was thinking about my wife. I wasn't paying any attention.'

'Try to remember.'

'I am trying.'

'Someone, at a window, might have seen you passing.'

He was triumphant.

'There was a lighted window at the corner of the rue des Prémontrés and the rue des Deux-Ponts.'

'Whose house?'

'I don't know, but I could show it to you.'

'Was the window open?'

'No, I don't think so. The blind was lowered. I actually thought of an invalid . . .'

'Why an invalid?'

'No particular reason. It was all so quiet . . .'

Basquin was watching him gravely, without severity, without antipathy. On his side, Jonas found it natural that he should be doing his duty and preferred it to be him than anyone else. The inspector was sure to understand sooner or later.

'It has happened before that Gina . . .' he began shame-facedly.

'I know. But she's never been away four days before, has she? And there was always someone who knew where she was.'

What did he mean by that? That when she went on a spree Gina kept some people informed, her brother, for example, or one of her friends, like Clémence? Basquin had not just spoken idly. He knew what he was talking about, seemed to know more about it than even Jonas himself.

'Did you have a quarrel on Wednesday?'

'We never quarrelled, I promise you.'

Madame Lallemand, the mother of the young cripple, came in to exchange her two books and the conversation was left in suspense. Had she heard any rumours? She appeared to know the inspector, at any rate to know who he was, for she looked embarrassed and said:

'Give me anything of the same kind.'

Had she realized that it was an actual interrogation that the bookseller was undergoing? She left hurriedly like someone who realizes they are not wanted and in the meantime Basquin, having replaced his book on the shelf, had lit a cigarette.

'Not even,' he resumed, 'when she had spent the night out?'

Jonas said forcefully:

'Not even then. I never even reproached her.'

He saw the policeman frown and realized that it was hard to believe. Yet he was speaking the truth.

'You are asking me to believe that it made no difference to you?'

'It did hurt me.'

'And you avoided showing it?'

It was genuine curiosity which had perhaps nothing professional about it, that he read in Basquin's eyes, and he would have liked to make him understand exactly how he felt. His face was covered with sweat and his spectacles were beginning to mist over.

'I didn't need to show it to her. She knew it already. In actual fact she was ashamed, but she wouldn't have let it be seen for anything in this world.'

'Gina was ashamed?'

Raising his head he almost cried out, he was so sure that he was right:

'Yes! And it would have been cruel to add to her shame. It wouldn't have been any good. Don't you understand? She couldn't help it. It was in her nature . . .'

Stupefied, the inspector was watching him speak, and for a moment Jonas hoped he had convinced him.

'I had no right to reproach her.'

'You are her husband.'

He sighed wearily:

'Of course . . .'

He realized that his hopes had been premature.

'How many times did it happen in the past two years? For it was two years ago that you got married, wasn't it?'

'Two years ago last month. I haven't counted the number of times.'

It wasn't entirely true. He could have remembered it in a few moments, but it was not important and the question reminded him of the ones the priest asks in the confessional.

'The last time?'

'Six months ago.'

'Did you know who it was with?'

He raised his voice again.

'No! No! Why should I want to know?'

How could it have helped him, to know the man Gina had slept with? To have even more vivid pictures in his mind and suffer all the more?

'You love her?'

He replied almost in a whisper:

'Yes.'

It made him wince to talk about it, because it concerned no one but himself.

'In short, you love her but you're not jealous.'

It wasn't a question. It was a conclusion, and he did not take it up. He was discouraged. It was no longer the more or less marked coldness of the market people that he was up against, but the reasoning of a man who, on account of his profession, ought to have been capable at least of understanding.

'You're sure Gina left the house on Wednesday evening?'

'Yes.'

'At what time?'

'Directly after dinner. She washed up, but forgot to clean the stove, and told me she was going round to the Reverdis.'

'Did she go up to her room?'

'I think so. Yes.'

'You aren't sure?'

'Yes, I am. I remember now.'

'Did she stay there long?'

'Not very long.'

'Did you see her to the door?'

'Yes.'

'So you saw which way she went?'

'Towards the rue des Prémontrés.'

He pictured in his mind's eye the red of her dress in the grey light of the street.

'You're sure your wife didn't spend the night of Wednesday to Thursday here?'

He reddened again as he said:

'Certain.'

And he was about to open his mouth to explain, for he was intelligent enough to know what was coming next. Basquin was too quick for him.

'Yet you told her father that she had taken the bus to Bourges, at 7.10 on Thursday morning.'

'I know. It was wrong.'

'You were lying?'

'It wasn't exactly a lie.'

'You repeated it to different people and you gave details.'

'I was just going to explain . . .'

'Answer my question first. Had you any reason for hiding from Palestri the fact that his daughter had gone off on Wednesday evening?'

'No.'

He hadn't had any particular reason for hiding it from Louis, and besides, that was not how it had all started. If only he could have a chance to tell the story the way it had happened, there would be some hope of being understood.

'You admit that Palestri knew all about his daughter's conduct?'

'I think so . . . Yes . . .'

'Angèle as well . . . She certainly didn't make any secret of it . . .'

He could have wept at his own impotence.

'It's no use pretending that Gina was ashamed, she never tried to hide it herself, quite the opposite.'

'That's not the same thing. It isn't that sort of shame.'

'What sort is it?'

He was tempted to give up, from weariness. They were two intelligent men face to face, but they didn't speak the same language and they were on completely different planes.

'It was all the same to her what people said. It was . . .'

He wanted to explain that it was in regard to herself that she was ashamed, but he was not being given the chance.

'And to you, was it all the same to you?'

'Of course it was!'

The words had been faster than his thoughts. It was true and yet untrue. He realized that that was going to contradict what he had still to explain.

'So you had no reason to hide the fact that she had gone?'

'I didn't hide it.'

His throat was dry, his eyes smarted.

'What difference,' went on Basquin without giving him a chance to go back on what he had said, 'would it make whether she left on Wednesday evening or Thursday morning?'

'Exactly.'

'Exactly what?'

'It doesn't make any difference. That proves that I wasn't really lying.'

'When you said that your wife had taken the bus at 7.10 to go and see La Loute at Bourges? And in repeating it to at least six people, including your mother-in-law?'

'Listen, Monsieur Basquin . . .'

'I am only too anxious to listen.'

It was true. He was trying to understand, but even so there was in Jonas's manner something which was beginning to irritate him. Jonas noticed it, and that made him lose his bearings even more. As at Le Bouc's during the last few days, there was a wall between himself and the other man, and he was beginning to wonder if he was like other men.

'I was hoping that Gina would come back on Thursday in the morning.'

'Why?'

'Because, most times, she only used to go away for the night.'

It hurt him to say it, but he was ready to suffer more than that for the sake of being left in peace.

'When I saw that she didn't come, I told myself that she would be back during the day and I carried on as if nothing had happened.'

'Why?'

'Because it wasn't worth the bother of . . .'

Would someone else have behaved differently in his place? He had to take advantage of the fact that he was being allowed to get a few words in.

'I went into Le Bouc's around ten o'clock, as I do every day.'

'And you announced that your wife had left for Bourges by the morning bus to go and see her friend.'

Jonas lost his temper, stamped his foot, shouted:

'No!'

'You didn't say so in the presence of five or six witnesses?'

'Not like that. It's not the same thing. Le Bouc asked me how Gina was and I replied that she was all right. Ancel, who was near me, can confirm it. I think it was also Fernand who remarked that he hadn't seen her at the market that morning.'

'What difference does that make?'

'Wait!' he begged. 'It was then that I said she had gone to Bourges.'

'Why?'

'To explain her absence and give her time to come back without there being any fuss.'

'You said just now that it was all the same to her.'

He shrugged his shoulders. He had said so, certainly.

'And that it was all the same to you as well . . .'

'Let's say I was caught off my guard. I was in a bar, surrounded by acquaintances, and they were asking me where my wife was.'

'They asked you *where* she was?'

'They mentioned that they had not seen her. I replied that she had gone to Bourges.'

'Why Bourges?'

'Because she used occasionally to go there.'

'And why mention the 7.10 bus?'

'Because I remembered that there wasn't a bus to Bourges in the evening.'

'You thought of everything.'

'I thought of that by chance.'

'And La Loute?'

'I don't even think I was the first to mention her. If I remember rightly, Le Bouc said, "Has she gone to see La Loute?" Because everyone knows that La Loute is at Bourges and that Gina and she are friends.'

'Strange!' murmured Basquin, looking at him more closely than ever.

'It's all quite simple,' answered Jonas, forcing a smile.

'Perhaps it isn't as simple as all that!'

And the inspector pronounced these words in a grave tone, with an expression of annoyance on his face.

Chapter Six

Was Basquin hoping that Jonas would change his mind and make a confession? Or was he simply anxious to underline the unofficial character of his visit? Whatever the case, he behaved before leaving as he had done on his entry, like a customer who has dropped in, glancing through a few books with his back turned to the bookseller.

Finally he looked at his watch, sighed, picked up his hat from the chair.

'It's time I was getting along. No doubt we shall have another opportunity to talk all this over again.'

He did not say it as a threat, but as if the two of them had a problem to solve.

Jonas followed him to the door, which had been open all the time, and with a reflex action common to all shopkeepers, glanced up and down the street. He was still shaken. The sun shone full upon him when he turned to the right and he could not make out the faces around Angèle. What he was sure of was that there was a group on the pavement, round the greengrocer's wife, most of them women, and that everybody was looking in his direction.

Turning to the left, he caught sight of another group, in Le Bouc's doorway with, as a focal point, Ancel's working overalls with their narrow blue and white stripes and his bloodstained apron.

So they had known what was going on ahead of him and had

been keeping an eye open for the inspector's visit. Through the wide-open door of the shop they must have caught fragments of conversation, when Jonas had raised his voice. Perhaps some of them had even approached softly without being noticed?

He was even more shocked than he was frightened by the thought. They were not behaving decently to him and he did not deserve it. He was ashamed of giving the impression of running away or retreating abruptly into his shop, but there and then, without warning, he was in no fit state to face their hostile curiosity.

For that their silence was hostile there could be no doubt. He would have preferred whistles and insults.

Well, this was the silence that he was going to have to endure for the next few days, during which he lived as if in a universe detached from the rest of the world.

He made himself go on with his work, without realizing precisely what he was doing, and, a few minutes before four o'clock, instinct made him look at his watch. It was time for his cup of coffee at Le Bouc's. Was he going to change his routine? He was tempted to do so. That was the simplest solution. But in spite of everything that Basquin might think, it was from loyalty to Gina, it was for Gina's sake that he was so anxious for life to continue as before.

When he came out of the door, there was no longer anybody spying on him, and the Chaignes's red-haired dog, which had been sleeping in the sun, struggled lazily to its feet and came over to sniff his heels and offer its head to be patted.

In Le Bouc's bar he found only a stranger, and the old beggar-woman who was eating a hunk of bread and a piece of sausage in a corner.

''Afternoon, Fernand. An espresso coffee, please,' he said, carefully noting the inflexions of his own voice.

He was striving to remain natural. Without a word, Fernand placed a cup under the chromium tap and let the steam escape, avoiding his eyes, ill at ease, as if he were not convinced that they weren't all behaving rather cruelly.

He couldn't act differently from the others. Jonas understood that. All the Old Market, at the moment, was forming a bloc against him, including, in all likelihood, people who didn't know anything about the affair.

He didn't deserve it, not only because he was innocent of everything they might accuse him of, but because he had always tried, discreetly, quietly, to live like them, with them, and to be like them.

He believed, only a few days before, that he had succeeded by dint of patience and humility. For he had been humble as well. He did not lose sight of the fact that he was a foreigner, a member of another race, born in far-off Archangel, whom the fortunes of wars and revolutions had transplanted to a small town in the Berry.

Shepilov, for instance, did not possess this humility. Having fled to France, he did not think twice before taking it on himself to criticize the country and its customs, even its politics, and Constantin Milk himself, when he had his fishmonger's shop, did not hesitate to talk to Natalie in Russian in front of the customers.

No one had resented it, in his case. Was it because he had asked nothing and did not worry about what his neighbours thought? The ones who had known him talked of him still with affection, as of a strong and colourful personality.

Jonas, perhaps because his first conscious memories had been of the Vieux-Marché, had always tried to become integrated. He did not ask the people to recognize him as one of themselves. He felt that that was impossible. He behaved with the discretion of a guest, and it was as a guest that he saw himself.

They had let him be, let him open his shop. In the morning they called out their ritual:

' 'Morning, Monsieur Jonas!'

There had been about thirty of them at his wedding reception, and outside the church the whole of the market had ranged themselves in two rows on the steps.

Why were they suddenly changing their attitude?

He would have sworn that things would not have turned out the same if what had happened to him had happened to one of themselves. He had become a foreigner again overnight, a man from another clan, from another world, come to eat their bread and take one of their daughters.

It did not anger him, nor embitter him, but it caused him pain, and like Basquin, he, too, repeated insistently:

'Why?'

It was hard to be there, at Fernand's bar, which was like a second home to him, and see the latter silent, distant, to be obliged to remain silent himself.

He didn't ask what he owed, as he had done last time, but put the money down on the linoleum of the counter.

'Good night, Fernand.'

'Good night.'

Not the usual:

'*Good night, Monsieur Jonas.*'

Only a vague and cold:

'*Good night.*'

It was Monday, and this was to go on for four days, until the Friday. Gina sent no word of herself. There was nothing about her in any of the papers. At one moment he thought that Marcel might have escaped and that she had rejoined him, but an escape would probably have attracted a certain amount of publicity.

During those four days he managed, by sheer will-power, to remain the same, rose every morning at the usual time, went across to the other side of the Square for his three croissants, made his coffee, then, a little later in the morning, went up to do his room.

At ten o'clock he would go into Le Bouc's, and when Louis was there one time, on the Wednesday, he had the strength of mind not to retreat. He was expecting to be harangued by Palestri, who had already had a few drinks. On the contrary, he was greeted by an absolute silence; on seeing him everyone stopped talking, except for a stranger who was talking to Le Bouc and who uttered another remark or two, looking round him in surprise, only to end up in an embarrassed silence.

Each day at noon he went round to Pepito's, and neither he nor his niece once engaged him in conversation. The Widower went on blinking his eyelids, but then hadn't he, too, been living in a world of his own for a long time?

Customers still came to his shop, fewer than usual, and he did not see Madame Lallemand, whose daughter ought to have finished her last two books.

Often two whole hours would pass without anyone coming in through the doorway, and to keep himself occupied, he undertook the cleaning of his shelves, one by one, dusting book after book, so that he came across various works which had been there for years and which he had forgotten about.

He spent hours thus occupied on his bamboo steps, seeing the Square outside now deserted, now enlivened with the colourful bustle of the market.

He hadn't spoken to Basquin about the missing stamps. Was that going to recoil upon him too? The Inspector had only asked him whether Gina had any money, and he had replied that she could not have had much, which was true.

He, too, was beginning to be afraid that some accident had befallen Gina. Once at least, he was sure, she had spent the night in a squalid furnished room in the rue Haute, with a North African. Mightn't she have fallen this time on a sadist or a madman, or one of those desperadoes who kill for a few hundred francs?

It comforted him to think that she had taken the stamps for it enabled him almost for sure to dismiss this theory.

He felt so alone, so helpless, that he was tempted to go and seek the advice of the Abbé Grimault, in the tranquillity of his parlour, where the smell and the semi-obscurity were so soothing. What could the priest have said to him? Why should he understand any better than Basquin, who at least had a wife himself?

In the evening he made his supper, did the washing-up. He did not again touch the album of Russian stamps, which reminded him that he was of another race. He was feeling almost guilty, by now, for having amassed this collection as if it were an act of treason towards the people amongst whom he lived.

However, it was not from patriotism or nostalgia for a country which he did not know, that he had gathered all these stamps together. He could not have said exactly what impulse he had obeyed. Perhaps it was because of Doussia? He had talked about her to Gina, one Sunday afternoon, in the back-yard, and Gina had asked:

'Is she older than you?'

'She was two when I was born. She would be forty-two now.'

'Why do you say *would be*?'

'Because she may be dead.'

'Did they kill children so young?'

'I don't know. It's possible that she's still alive.'

She had looked at him wonderingly.

'How strange!' she had murmured finally.

'What?'

'Everything. You. Your family. Your sisters. All these people who are perhaps living quietly over there without your knowing it and may very well be wondering what's happened to you. Haven't you ever wanted to go and see them?'

'No.'

'Why not?'

'I don't know.'

She hadn't understood and she must have thought that he had disowned his family. It wasn't true.

'Do you think they shot your father?'

'They may have sent him to Siberia. Perhaps again they've let him go back to Archangel.'

How ironical if all the family had been reunited out there in their town, in their own house – who could say? All except him!

On one occasion he found himself next to Constable Benaiche at Le Bouc's bar and Benaiche pretended not to see him. Now though he went three times a week to the market on duty, he was not part of the market and he must know what they thought of Jonas at the police station.

Basquin had given him to understand that they would be meeting again, and Jonas was hourly expecting his arrival. He had forced himself to prepare answers to the questions he anticipated. He had even summarized, on a scrap of paper, his movements on the Thursday, the day he had talked so much about the visit to Bourges, with a list of people he had spoken to.

Four days of living as though in a glass frame, like certain animals on which experiments are being made in laboratories and which are observed hour by hour. There was a violent storm on the Thursday morning, when the market was at its height, which caused a stampede, for the rain fell in huge drops mixed with hailstones, and two women he didn't know took refuge in his shop. The downpour lasted nearly an hour and activities outside were almost suspended; he was himself unable to go to Le Bouc's at ten o'clock and it was about half past eleven before he went to have his coffee in the bar, which smelt of damp wool.

He was still compelling himself to say, as usual, as if nothing had happened:

'Morning, Fernand.'

And he ordered his coffee, while unwrapping his two pieces of sugar.

That afternoon, towards five o'clock, a policeman on a bicycle stopped outside the shop and came in, leaving his machine propped up at the edge of the pavement.

'You are Jonas Milk?'

He said yes, and the man handed him a yellow envelope, then a notebook like the ones postmen used for registered packages.

'Sign here.'

He signed, waited until he was alone again before opening the envelope, which contained an official letter printed on coarse paper, summoning him to the police station for the following day, Friday, at ten o'clock in the morning.

They were not going to continue coming to question him with an air of casually passing by. They were summoning him. On the dotted line following the word 'Reason' there was written in indelible pencil:

'*Personal Matters.*'

He felt a desire, that evening, to put in writing all that had happened since the Wednesday evening, and in particular, during the whole of Thursday, with a sincere explanation of every one of his actions, every one of his words, but it was in vain that he sat at his desk and tried to decide where to start.

They had not yet accused him of anything whatsoever. They had merely asked him insidious questions and created a vacuum around him.

Perhaps it would be better after all for him at last to have an opportunity to explain everything from beginning to end. He did not know who, over there, would see him. The summons was signed by the superintendent, whom he knew by sight. He was called Devaux and, if only from the hair in his nostrils and ears, he looked like Monsieur Métras. He was a widower, too, lived with his daughter who had married a young doctor from Saint-Amand, with a house in the rue Gambetta.

He slept badly, woke up almost every hour, had confused nightmares, and dreamed, among other things, of the canal and the lock-gate, which had been raised to allow a barge to pass and which would not go down again. Why was he to blame? It was a mystery, but everybody was accusing him and he had been given a ridiculously short time to make the bridge work; he was bathed in sweat, gripping the operating handle with his hands, while Ancel, who was carrying a quarter of beef on his shoulder, was sneering at him.

They were treating him like a convict. That is what emerged clearly from his dream. There was also some talk of Siberia.

'You who come from Siberia . . .'

He endeavoured to explain that Archangel is not in Siberia, but they knew better than he did. Siberia, God knows why, had something to do with the fact that he was the person who had to turn the handle, and Madame Lentin came into it too, he could not recall how, perhaps because he remembered her pale face behind her lace window curtains.

He was almost afraid to go back to sleep, so much did these nightmares exhaust him, and at five o'clock in the morning he preferred to get up and go out in the street for some air.

In this way he reached the Square outside the station, where there was a bar open, and he had a cup of coffee and ate some croissants which had just arrived and were still warm. Would the baker's wife be surprised when he did not come for his three croissants as on other days? He passed by the bus station, too, where two large green coaches, one of them for Bourges, were waiting for the time to go, without anyone in them.

At eight o'clock he opened his shop, carried out the two boxes, took them in again at half past nine and then, with his hat on his head, his summons in his pocket, he went out and locked his shop.

It was not quite time to go to Le Bouc's, but since he would be at the police station at ten o'clock, he went in and drank his coffee.

They must have noticed his hat. They must have seen, too, that he locked his door. However, they did not ask him any questions, but ignored him as they had ignored him for the past four days. Nevertheless he said:

'See you later.'

He took the rue Haute. About 500 yards up on the left there was a square, in the middle of which stood the grey building of the Town Hall.

Here also there was a market, much less important than the one opposite his shop, a few barrows of vegetables and fruit, two or three stalls, a woman selling baskets and bootlaces.

To reach the police station one did not go in by the main entrance but by a small door in the side street, and he went into the first room which smelled like a barracks and was divided in two by a sort of black wooden counter.

Five or six people were waiting on a bench and, out of humility or timidity, he was going to sit in the queue, when a police sergeant called to him:

'What do you want?'

He stammered:

'I've had a summons.'

'Let's see.'

He glanced at it, disappeared through a door, and said on returning a little later:

'Wait a minute.'

Jonas remained standing to start off with, and the hands of the clock, on the rough white wall, pointed to ten past ten, a quarter past ten, twenty past ten. Then he sat down, fiddling with his hat, wondering whether, as at the doctor's, all the people ahead of him had to go in first.

It was not the case, for when they called a name, a woman

rose and was led in the opposite direction to the one the sergeant had taken a short time before. Then they said another name and told an elderly man who was going towards the desk:

'Sign here ... Now here ... You've got four hundred and twenty-two francs?'

He held the money in his hand and, in exchange, was given a pink piece of paper which he folded carefully and put in his wallet before leaving.

'Next!'

It was an old woman, who leaned towards the sergeant and spoke to him in a low voice, and Jonas was unconsciously straining his ears to hear, when a bell rang.

'One moment!' the man in uniform interrupted her. 'Monsieur Milk! This way please.'

He went down a corridor on to which there opened a number of offices, until he came to the one where the superintendent, sitting in front of a piece of mahogany furniture, had his back to the window.

'Sit down,' he said, without looking up.

He wore spectacles for reading and writing, which Jonas did not know, only having seen him in the street, and he took them off each time he looked at him.

'Your name is Jonas Milk, born at Archangel on 21 September 1916, naturalized a Frenchman on 17 May 1938?'

'Yes, superintendent.'

The man had in front of him some closely written sheets of paper which he appeared to be perusing in order to refresh his memory.

'Two years ago you married Eugénie Louise Joséphine Palestri.'

He nodded his head and the superintendent leaned back in his chair, played with his spectacles for a moment, before asking him:

'Where is your wife, Monsieur Milk?'

To hear himself addressed by that name, to which he had become unaccustomed, was enough to discompose him.

'I don't know, superintendent.'

'I see here' – and he tapped the papers in front of him with his horn-rimmed spectacles, which he had folded up – 'that you have provided at least two different accounts of her departure.'

'Let me explain.'

'One moment. On the one hand, to several of your neighbours you declared spontaneously and in the presence of witnesses, on Thursday morning, then on Thursday afternoon and on Friday, that your wife had left the town by the 7.10 bus.'

'That is correct.'

'She did take the bus?'

'No. It is correct that I said so.'

It was starting all over again. The huge sheets of official paper contained the report from Inspector Basquin, who must have, back in his office, reconstructed their conversation from memory.

'On the other hand, when you were questioned afterwards by one of my colleagues, you changed your wife's departure to Wednesday evening.'

As he was opening his mouth, a sharp rap of the glasses on the dossier interrupted him.

'One moment, Monsieur Milk, I am bound to warn you first that we have been requested to start a search for her as a missing person.'

Was it Louis who had come and asked for this? Or Angèle? Or Frédo? He didn't dare inquire, although he was burning to know.

'These affairs are always delicate, especially when it concerns a woman, and, even more so, a married woman. I summoned you to ask you a certain number of questions and I shall be obliged to go into somewhat intimate details. It is understood that I am not accusing you of anything and you have the right not to reply.'

'I only ask to . . .'

'Please let me do the talking. I shall first of all outline the position as briefly as possible.'

He put on his spectacles, looked for another piece of paper on which he had apparently jotted down a few notes.

'You are forty years old and your wife, better known under the name of Gina, is twenty-four. If I understand rightly, she did not pass for a model of virtue before she met you and, as a neighbour, you were aware of her conduct. Is that correct?'

'That is correct.'

Life, described thus, in official language, how odious it became!

'Nevertheless you married her, in the full knowledge of the facts and, in order that the wedding should take place in church, a condition without which the Palestris would not have given their consent, you became converted to Catholicism and were baptized.'

This was another shock, for it revealed that an intensive inquiry had been going on about him during the empty days he had just passed. Had they been to question the Abbé Grimault, and others as well, whose names were perhaps yet to emerge?

'By the way, Monsieur Milk, I should like to ask you a question which has nothing to do with this matter. You are a Jew, I believe?'

For the first time he replied as if he were ashamed of it:

'Yes.'

'You were here during the occupation?'

'Yes.'

'So you remember that at one time the German authorities made it compulsory for your co-religionists to wear a yellow star on their clothes?'

'Yes.'

'How is it that you never wore this star and yet did not get into trouble?'

In order to remain calm he had to dig his nails into the palms of his hands.

What could he reply? Was he to renounce his own people? He had never felt himself to be a Jew. He had never believed himself to be different from the people who surrounded him at the Old Market and they, just because of his fair hair and blue eyes, had never thought that he was of another race.

It was not in order to deceive them that he had not worn the yellow star, at the risk of being sent to a concentration camp or condemned to death. He had taken the risk, naturally, because he wanted to remain like the others.

The superintendent, who did not know him, had not found all this out on his own. Nor was it Basquin, who at the time was a prisoner-of-war in Germany.

It had come from somebody else, from somebody at the market, one of the people who used to give him a friendly greeting every morning.

'Did your wife know that you were a Jew?'

'I never talked about it to her.'

'Do you think that would have affected her decision?'

'I don't think so.'

As he said it, he thought bitterly of the Arab with whom she had once spent the night.

'And her parents?'

'It never occurred to me to wonder.'

'Let's leave that on one side. Do you speak German?'

'No.'

'Russian, of course?'

'I used to speak it once, with my parents, but I have forgotten it and I could hardly even understand it now.'

What had this to do with the disappearance of Gina? Was he finally going to discover what they had against him?

'Your father came to France as an émigré, at the time of the Revolution.'

'He was a prisoner in Germany and when the armistice was signed, in 1918 . . .'

'Let's call him an émigré, since at that time he did not return to Russia. I suppose he formed part of some White Russian group?'

He seemed to remember that at first Shepilov had made him a member of some political society, but Constantin Milk had never been an active member and had dedicated himself entirely to his fishmonger's business.

Without waiting for his answer, Superintendent Devaux went on:

'Yet in 1930 he did not hesitate to go back to his country. Why?'

'To find out what had become of my five sisters.'

'Did you hear any news of him?'

'Never.'

'Not a letter, or by word of mouth, or through friends?'

'In no way at all.'

'How is it, in that case, that your mother went off in her turn?'

'Because she could not live without her husband.'

'Have you ever indulged in political activities?'

'Never.'

'You don't belong to any group, or party?'

'No.'

Devaux put on his spectacles to consult his notes once again. He looked put out. One would have said that it was only with a certain reluctance that he was asking certain questions.

'You carry on a considerable correspondence with foreign countries, Monsieur Milk.'

Had they questioned the postman as well? Who else?

'I am a philatelist.'

'Does that call for such an extensive foreign correspondence?'

'Given my method of work, yes.'

He felt the desire to explain the mechanics of his operations,
the research work among the raw material which he had sent
to him from the four corners of the earth, for stamps with
peculiarities which had escaped his colleagues.

'We'll leave that on one side,' the superintendent said once
again, apparently in a hurry to get to the end of the interview.

Nevertheless he added:

'How are your relations with your neighbours?'

'Good. Very good. I mean up to the last few days.'

'What has happened in the last few days?'

'They have been avoiding me.'

'You received, I believe, a visit from your brother-in-law,
Alfred Palestri, known as Frédo?'

'Yes.'

'What do you think of him?'

He said nothing.

'Are you on bad terms?'

'I don't think he likes me.'

'For what reason?'

'Perhaps he wasn't pleased that I married his sister.'

'And your father-in-law?'

'I don't know.'

After a glance at his notes, the superintendent resumed:

'It would appear that both of them were opposed to your
marriage. Gina, at the time, was in your service, if I am not
mistaken?'

'She was working in my house as my servant.'

'Did she sleep in the house?'

'No.'

'Did you have intimate relations with her?'

'Not before we were married.'

'The idea of starting a family never came to you before?'

'No.'

It was true. It had never occurred to him.

'I am going, for my own guidance, to ask you another indiscreet question and you are perfectly entitled to refuse to answer. How did you manage?'

He did not understand at once. The superintendent had to elucidate:

'A man has his needs . . .'

Before the war there was a house, not far from the Town Hall, in the rue du Pot-de-Fer to be precise, which Jonas visited regularly. The new laws had upset his arrangements for a time, then he had discovered a street corner, near the station, where four or five women walked their beat of an evening in front of a private hotel.

He admitted to it, since he was in any case being forced to strip his soul bare.

'According to what you said, you were not jealous of your wife?'

'I didn't say that. I said I did not let her see it.'

'I understand. So you were jealous?'

'Yes.'

'What would you have done if you had caught her in the arms of another man?'

'Nothing.'

'You wouldn't have been furious?'

'I should have suffered.'

'But you wouldn't have used violence, either against her or against her partner?'

'Certainly not.'

'Did she know that?'

'She must have known it.'

'Did she take advantage of the fact?'

He felt like replying:

'It's all written down in front of you!'

But if he had already been overawed once when Inspector Basquin had interrogated him in his shop, which he had entered with the casual air of a customer, he was very much more so in this formal office where, on top of everything else, they had just touched on sensitive points, and left him as if he had been flayed alive.

There were words, sentences, which went on resounding in his head and he had to make an effort to understand what was being said to him.

'You never threatened her?'

He started.

'What with?'

'I don't know. You never uttered any threat against her?'

'Never in my life. It would never have occurred to me to do so!'

'Not even during a quarrel at home, for example, or perhaps after a few drinks?'

'We never had any quarrels and you must have been told that I only drink coffee.'

The superintendent slowly lit his pipe, which he had been filling, and leant back in his armchair, his spectacles in his hand.

'In that case, how can you explain that your wife is frightened of you?'

He thought he had misheard him.

'What did you say?'

'I said "that she is frightened of you".'

'Gina?'

'Your wife, yes.'

He started to his feet, overawed though he was by his surroundings. It was with some difficulty that he was able to pronounce clearly the words that came, in a confused torrent, to his lips.

'But, superintendent, she was never frightened of me . . . Frightened of what? . . . When she came back, on the contrary, I . . .'

'Sit down.'

He was twisting his hands together. It was meaningless, as if he was living one of his nightmares of the night before.

'Afraid of me!' he repeated. 'Of me!'

Whoever could be afraid of him? Not even the stray dogs of the market, or the cats. He was the most inoffensive being on the face of the earth.

The superintendent, meanwhile, who had put his spectacles on again, ran his eyes over a report while his fingers underlined a passage.

'On several occasions, your wife declared that you would end up by killing her.'

'When? Who to? It's not possible.'

'I am not at liberty, at present, to disclose the name of the person to whom she made these confidences, but I can assure you that she made them, and not just to one person.'

Jonas was capitulating. It was too much. They had just gone too far. That the neighbours had turned against him he could endure, by gritting his teeth.

But that Gina . . .

'Listen, superintendent . . .'

He stretched out his hands in supplication, in a final outburst of energy.

'If she was afraid of me, why . . . ?'

What was the use? In any case, the words failed him. He had forgotten what he was going to say. It no longer mattered.

Afraid of him!

'Keep calm. Once again I am not accusing you of anything. An inquiry has been opened as a result of your wife's disappearance and it is my duty not to neglect anything, to listen to all the evidence.'

Without realizing, he nodded his approval.

'The fact is that for some mysterious reason, ever since the morning when your wife's disappearance was noted, you have been lying.'

He did not protest, as he had done with Inspector Basquin.

'Afraid of me!' he kept repeating to himself with bitter obstinacy.

'This has inevitably given rise to certain rumours.'

His head went on nodding affirmatively.

'All I am asking is to clear the matter up with your help.'

The face and outline of the superintendent suddenly danced in front of his eyes and he felt himself being overcome by a weakness which he had never known before.

'You . . . you haven't a glass of water?' he had time to stammer.

It was the first time in his life that he had fainted. It was very hot in the room. The superintendent rushed to the door and Jonas had time to hear water flowing from a tap.

He could not have been unconscious for more than a few seconds, for when he opened his eyes, the glass was clinking against his teeth and the cold water was trickling down his chin.

He looked without resentment, his eyes half-closed, at the man who had just caused him so much pain, who now stood bending over him.

'Do you feel better?'

He blinked his eyelids, as he did to greet the Widower, who was rather like the superintendent to look at. Perhaps after all the superintendent was a decent fellow and was sorry for him?

'Have another drink.'

He shook his head. He was embarrassed. A nervous reaction made him suddenly feel like crying. He mastered himself, but it was a good minute before he was able to speak. Then it was to stammer:

'I am sorry.'

'Relax and keep quiet.'

The superintendent opened the window, suddenly letting in the noises from the street, went and sat down in his place again, not knowing what to do or say.

Chapter Seven

'I don't think, Monsieur Milk,' the superintendent was saying, 'that you have quite grasped the point. Once again, for some reason or other, your wife has disappeared, and we have been asked to investigate. We have had no choice but to collect statements and check certain rumours which were circulating.'

Jonas was calm again now, too calm, and the smile on his face looked as if an india-rubber could have wiped it away. He was looking at the other politely, his mind elsewhere; in actual fact he was listening to the crowing of a cock, which had just broken, strident and proud, into the noises from the street. At first it had surprised him so much that he had a feeling of unreality, of floating, until he recalled that just opposite the police station there was a man who dealt in birds and farmyard animals.

By rising from his chair he could have seen the cages piled on top of one another on the pavement, hens, cocks, and pedigree ducks underneath, then on top, parakeets, canaries and other birds, some bright red, others blue, whose names he did not know. To the right of the door, a parrot stood on its perch and passers-by were constantly amazed that it was not attached.

In the Square a woman with a shrill voice, a costermonger, was calling on the world at large to buy her fine salads and the intervals in her monotonous cry were roughly regular, so that he ended up by waiting for it.

'I went about it a bit brutally, perhaps, and I am sorry . . .'

Jonas shook his head as if to say that all was well.

Gina was frightened of him. The rest did not matter. He could stand up to anything now, and the superintendent had no need to approach the question in a roundabout way.

'I will not conceal from you that there is another somewhat disturbing piece of evidence. On Wednesday, shortly before midnight, a woman was leaning out of her window, in the Rue du Canal, a quarter of a mile from where you live. She was waiting for her husband who, for reasons that need not concern us, had not returned home at the usual time. Anyway, she saw a rather small man, about your size, who was carrying a large sack on his shoulder, heading towards the lock and keeping close to the wall.'

'Did she recognize me?'

He was not angry, or indignant.

'I did not say that, but clearly it is a coincidence.'

'Do you think, superintendent, that I would have had the strength to carry my wife from the Place du Vieux-Marché to the canal?'

If Gina was very little bigger than he was, she was heavier and he was not a strong man.

Monsieur Devaux bit his lips. Since Jonas had fainted, he was less at his ease and was minding how he went, without realizing that it was no longer necessary. Isn't there a moment when the intensity of pain brings on insensitivity? Jonas had passed that crisis and, while he listened to what was being said, he was concentrating on the noises from the street.

It wasn't the same sound as in his quarter. The cars were more frequent, the pedestrians in more of a hurry. The light itself was different, and yet it was not ten minutes' walk from here to the Vieux-Marché.

The cupboards, behind the superintendent, were made of mahogany like the desk, with green baize cloth stretched behind gold-coloured lattice work, and above, in a wooden frame, could be seen a photograph of the President of the Republic.

'I thought of that objection, Monsieur Milk. But you are not unaware, if you read the papers, that this problem has often, alas, been overcome.'

He did not understand straight away.

'You cannot have failed to read or hear stories of dis-membered bodies being found in rivers or waste land. Once again, I am not accusing you.'

He was not being accused of cutting Gina into pieces and carrying them into the canal!

'What we have to do now, unless your wife reappears or we find her, is to exculpate you from the affair, and therefore to study all the possibilities calmly.'

He was replacing his spectacles in order to cast an eye over his notes.

'Why, after her disappearance, were you in such a hurry to take your washing and hers to the laundry?'

They knew his slightest acts, as if he had been living in a glass cage.

'Because it was laundry day.'

'Was it you who normally counted the washing and made up the parcel?'

'No.'

No and yes. Which proved how difficult it is to express an absolute truth. It was among Gina's duties, as in other households, and Gina usually attended to it. Only she never knew which day of the week it was and sometimes Jonas reminded her, while she was doing their room:

'Don't forget the laundry.'

It was also a habit of theirs to put the pillow-case with it under the counter, so as not to hold up the van driver, who was always in a hurry.

Gina lived in disorder. Indeed, had she not forgotten, before leaving, to wash the pan in which she had cooked the herrings? Jonas, who had lived alone a long time and had not always had a maid, had kept up the habit of thinking of everything and often, when Gina was away, of doing the chores she ought to have taken on.

'Your wife has just disappeared, Monsieur Milk. You told me a short while ago that you were in love with her. Yet you took the trouble to devote yourself to a job which men do not normally do.'

He could only repeat:

'It was laundry day.'

He felt that the other was examining him curiously. Basquin, too, had looked at him like that at certain moments, as a man who is trying to understand, but without success.

'You were not trying to hide compromising traces?'

'Traces of what?'

'On the Friday or the Saturday, you also turned out your kitchen.'

How often this had happened before Gina's day, when the maid was ill, and even after his marriage!

'These are details of no significance individually, I agree, but which added together are nothing if not disturbing.'

He nodded in agreement, a submissive schoolboy.

'You have no idea what liaisons your wife may have formed of late?'

'None.'

'Has she been away more often than usual?'

'No.'

As always in the morning, she would roam about the market, preferably in dressing-gown and slippers. In the afternoon she would probably dress, powder her face, put on scent and go and do her shopping in the town, or see one of her girl friends.

'Hasn't she received any letters either?'

'She never has had any letters at the house.'

'Do you think she received them somewhere else, at the poste restante, for example?'

'I don't know.'

'What you must admit is curious, seeing that you are an intelligent man, is that she should have gone off without taking any clothes, not even a coat and, according to your own statement, almost without any money. She didn't take a bus, nor the train, we have confirmed that.'

In the end he felt it better to mention the stamps. He was tired, he was in a hurry to get outside this office, and not have to listen to any more of these questions which had so little relation to reality.

'My wife,' he said, smarting at being finally driven to it, and with a sense of betrayal, 'had premeditated her departure.'

'How do you know, and why didn't you say so to Inspector Basquin?'

'In the wardrobe with the looking-glass in our bedroom there is a box which used to contain my rarest stamps.'

'Did she know about it?'

'Yes.'

'Are these stamps of any great value?'

'Several million francs.'

He wondered if he had been wise to speak, for the superintendent's reaction was not what he had expected. He was being looked at, not with incredulity, but with a hint of suspicion.

'You mean that you possessed several million francs' worth of stamps?'

'Yes. I began collecting them at school, when I was about thirteen, and I have never given it up.'

'Who, apart from your wife, has seen these stamps you possess?'

'Nobody.'

'So that you cannot prove that they were in the cupboard?'

He had become calm, patient, detached almost, as if it were no longer anything to do with Gina and himself, and that was perhaps because he was on professional ground.

'I can prove, as far as most of them are concerned, that I acquired them at a particular moment, either by purchase or by exchange, some of them fifteen years ago, some two or three years ago. Philatelists form a fairly small circle. It is nearly always known where the rarer specimens are to be found.'

'Excuse me interrupting you, Monsieur Milk. I know nothing about philately. I am trying, at present, to put myself in the position of a jury. You are saying that while still living in a manner which I would, with all due respect, describe as very modest, and I hope I don't offend you, you say that you had several millions' worth of stamps and that your wife has taken them away with her. You go on to say that as far as most of them are concerned, you are able to establish that they came into your possession a number of years ago. Is that correct?'

He nodded his head, listening to the cock which was crowing once more, and the superintendent, exasperated, got up to close the window.

'Do you mind?'

'As you wish.'

'The first question that will arise is whether, last Wednesday, these stamps were still in your possession, for there was nothing to stop you from reselling them a long time ago. Is it possible for you to prove this was not so?'

'No.'

'And can you prove that you have not still got them?'

'They are no longer in the box.'

'We are still in the realms of theory, aren't we? What was there to prevent you from having put them somewhere else?'

'Why should I?'

In order to incriminate Gina, that is what the superintendent was thinking. To make it seem that she had gone off taking his fortune with her.

'Do you see now how difficult and delicate my task is? The inhabitants of your neighbourhood, for some reason unknown to me, seem to have a grudge against you.'

'Up to these last few days, they have been very nice to me.'

The superintendent was studying him closely and Jonas found the explanation in his eyes. He did not understand either. Human beings of all sorts had been in and out of his office and he was accustomed to the most unusual kinds of confidences. But Jonas baffled him, and he could see him pass from sympathy to irritation, amounting at times to aversion, only to start again and try to find a fresh point of contact.

Had it not been the same with Basquin? Didn't that go to prove that he was not like other men? Would it have been different in the country where he was born, at Archangel, among the people of his own race?

All his life he had sensed it, intuitively. Even at school he made himself inconspicuous, as if in order to be forgotten, and he had been uncomfortable when, against his will, he came top in his class.

Hadn't they encouraged him to consider himself at home in the Vieux-Marché? Hadn't they suggested, at one moment, that he should join a shopkeepers' defence committee, and even become the treasurer? He had refused, feeling that it was not his place.

It was not without good reason that he had shown such humility. He could only assume that he had not shown enough, since they were turning against him.

'When did these stamps disappear, according to your story?'

'Normally I keep the key to the box in my pocket, with the key to the front door and the one for the till.'

He displayed the silver chain.

'On Wednesday morning I dressed as soon as I got up, but the day before I went down in my pyjamas.'

'So that your wife would have taken the stamps on the Tuesday morning?'

'I presume so.'

'Are they easy to sell?'

'No.'

'Well?'

'She doesn't know it. As I told you, dealers know one another. When a rare specimen is brought to them, they usually make inquiries about its origin.'

'Have you alerted your colleagues?'

'No.'

'For what reason?'

He shrugged his shoulders. He was beginning to sweat, and missed the noises from the street.

'So your wife went off without a coat, without luggage, but with a fortune she will not be able to realize. Is that right?'

He nodded.

'She left the Old Market on Wednesday evening, over a week ago now, and no one saw her go, no one saw her in the town, she didn't take the bus, nor the train: in short, she melted into thin air without leaving the slightest trace. Where, in your opinion, would she have the best chance of selling the stamps?'

'In Paris, obviously, or in a big city like Lyons, Bordeaux, Marseilles. Abroad, too.'

'Can you furnish me with a list of the stamp dealers in France?'

'The principal ones, yes.'

'I will send them a circular letter warning them. Now, Monsieur Milk . . .'

The superintendent rose to his feet, hesitated, as if he had not yet discharged the most disagreeable part of his task.

'It remains to me to ask your permission to instruct two of

my men to accompany you and pay a visit to your house. I could obtain a search warrant but, at this stage of the affair, I prefer to keep matters on a less official footing.'

Jonas had also risen to his feet. He had no reason for refusing since he had nothing to hide and since, in any case, he was not the stronger of the two.

'Now?'

'I should prefer it that way, yes.'

To prevent him from covering up traces?

It was at once laughable and tragic. All this had started with an innocent little remark:

'She has gone to Bourges'.

It was Le Bouc who, innocently too, had asked:

'On the bus?'

From there, little by little, there had grown ripples, then waves, which had invaded the market and finally reached as far as the police station, in the centre of the town.

He was no longer Monsieur Jonas, the bookseller in the Square whom everybody greeted cheerfully. For the super-intendent, and in the reports, he was Jonas Milk, born at Archangel, Russia, on 21 September 1916, naturalized French on 17 May 1938, exempted from military service, of Jewish origin, converted to Catholicism in 1954.

There remained one more facet of the affair to be revealed, which he was far from expecting. They were standing up. The conversation, or rather the interrogation, seemed to be at an end. Monsieur Devaux was playing with his spectacles, which now and then caught a ray from the sun.

'Anyway, Monsieur Milk, you have a simple way of establishing that these stamps were in your possession.'

He looked at him uncomprehendingly.

'They amount, you said, to a capital value of several million francs. They were bought from your income, and consequently it must be possible to find, in your income-tax returns, a record of the sum you invested. Naturally this does not concern me personally, and it falls in the province of the Direct Taxation authorities.'

They would corner him there, too, he knew in advance. He wouldn't be able to get them to accept a perfectly simple truth. He had never bought a stamp for 50,000 francs, or 100,000, or 300,000, even though he had possessed stamps of that value. He had discovered some by examining them with his magnifying glass, stamps whose rarity other people had failed to spot, and some of the others he had acquired by a series of exchanges.

As the superintendent had said, he lived very modestly.

What was the use of worrying about it, in the state he was already in? Only one thing counted. *Gina was afraid of him.* And, in the doorway of the office, he in his turn timidly asked a question.

'She really said I would kill her one day?'

'That is what emerges from the evidence.'

'To several people?'

'I can assure you so.'

'She didn't say why?'

Monsieur Devaux hesitated, reclosed the door, which he had just opened.

'Do you insist on my replying?'

'Yes.'

'You will note that I made no allusion to it during the course of the conversation. Twice, at least, when talking about you, she declared:

'*He's vicious.*'

He turned scarlet. This was the last word he had been expecting.

'Think about it, Monsieur Milk, and we will resume the discussion another day. For the present, Inspector Basquin will accompany you with one of his men.'

The superintendent's statement did not shock him, and he finally felt he was beginning to understand. Often Gina had watched him stealthily when he was busy, and when he raised his head, she had seemed confused. The look on her face was similar then to certain of Basquin's and the superintendent's looks.

All the same she lived with him. She saw him in all his behaviour, day and night.

Despite this, she had not grown used to it, and he remained an enigma to her.

She must have wondered, when she was still working with him as a maid, why he did not treat her as other men used to treat her, including Ancel. She was never overdressed and there was a wanton freedom in her movements which might have been taken as a provocation.

Had she thought him impotent, at that time, or did she attribute special tastes to him? Had she been the only one during the years to think so?

He could picture her, serious-faced, preoccupied, when he had spoken of marrying her. He could picture her undressing the first evening and calling to him as, fully dressed, he was pacing the room without daring to look at her.

'Aren't you going to undress?'

It was almost as if she was expecting to discover something abnormal about him. The truth was that he was ashamed of his over-pink, plump body.

She had turned down the bed, lain down with her knees apart, and watching him undress, as he was approaching awkwardly, she had exclaimed with a laugh, which in reality was perhaps just uneasiness:

'Are you going to keep your glasses on?'

He had taken them off. All the time he had lain upon her, he had felt that she was watching him, and she had not taken part, nor made any pretence at taking part in his pleasure.

'*You see!*' she had said.

What exactly did that mean? That, in spite of everything, he had got what he wanted? That, despite appearances, he was almost a normal man?

'Shall we go to sleep?'

'If you like.'

'Good night.'

She had not kissed him and he had not dared to do so either. The superintendent forced him to reflect that in two years they had never kissed. He had tried twice or three times and she had turned her head away, not abruptly, with no apparent revulsion.

Although they slept in the same bed, he approached her as seldom as possible, because she did not participate, and when, towards morning, he would hear her panting near to him, finally subsiding in the depths of the bed with a sigh that almost rent her in two, he used to keep his eyes closed and pretend to be asleep.

As the superintendent had just told him, they had not yet questioned him about that, but it would come.

What was it that frightened Gina?

Was it his calm, his gentleness, his abashed tenderness when she came back from one of her escapades? One would sometimes have said that she was defying him to beat her.

Would she then have been less afraid of him? Would she have stopped thinking of him as vicious?

'Basquin!' called the superintendent, who had moved towards the corridor.

In an office, Jonas saw the inspector at work in his shirtsleeves.

'Take somebody with you and accompany Monsieur Milk.'

'Right, superintendent.'

He must have known what he had to do, for he did not ask for instructions.

'Dambois!' he called out in his turn, addressing someone out of sight in another office.

Neither of them were in uniform but everyone, in the Old Market as in the town centre, knew them.

'Think it over, Monsieur Milk,' Monsieur Devaux was saying again by way of good-bye.

What he was thinking over was not what the superintendent imagined. He was no longer trying to defend himself, to reply to the more or less grotesque charges which they had levelled against him.

It was an inner debate which occupied his mind, a debate infinitely more tragic than their tale about a woman being cut up into pieces.

In a curious way they were right, but not in the way they imagined, and Jonas suddenly felt himself really guilty.

He had not effected Gina's disappearance or thrown her body into the canal.

He was not vicious either, in the sense they understood him to be, and he knew of no peculiarity in himself, no sexual abnormality.

He hadn't yet registered the point, for the revelation had been too recent, it had just come at the moment he least expected it, in the neutral atmosphere of an official building.

'Do you mind waiting for me a moment, Monsieur Jonas?'

Basquin went on giving the name he was used to, but it did not even please him any longer.

That stage was past. He had reached the office divided by a dark wooden counter where some new visitors were waiting on the bench, and he pretended, to keep up appearances, to be reading an official notice advertising the sale of some horses and oxen in the main square.

Wasn't it to her brother, to start with, that Gina had confided that she was frightened of him? Very probably. That explained Frédo's fierce opposition to the marriage.

Who else had she spoken to? Clémence? La Loute?

He tried to remember the words the superintendent had repeated to him:

'*That man will kill me one of these days . . .*'

Why? Because he did not react as she had expected when she ran after other men? Because he was too soft, too patient?

Did she think to herself that he was acting and that one day he would give free rein to his real instincts? He had told her, when he had talked to her about marriage:

'I can at least offer you *peace and quiet*.'

Those words or something like them. He had not talked to her of love, or happiness, but of peace and quiet, because he was too humble to imagine that he could give her anything else.

She was beautiful, full of vitality, and he was sixteen years older, a dusty, lonely little bookseller whose only passion in life was collecting stamps.

That was not entirely true. That was how it seemed, what people must think. The truth is that he lived intensely, in his inner self, a rich and varied life, the life of the entire Old Market, the entire neighbourhood, of which he knew the minutest movements.

Behind the shelter of his thick spectacles, which seemed to isolate him and give him an inoffensive air, was it not rather as if he had stolen the lives of the others, without their noticing it?

Was that what Gina had discovered on entering his house? Was that why she had spoken of vice and been afraid?

Did she hold it against him that he had bought her?

For he had bought her, he knew it and she knew it. Angèle knew it better than anyone, for she had sold her, and Louis as well, who had not dared to say anything for fear of his wife, and Frédo, who had revolted against it.

They had not sold her for money, but for peace and quiet.

He was so well aware of it that he had been the first to use the words as a bait, a temptation.

With him, Gina would have a front of respectability and her escapades would be covered up. Her material needs would be assured and Angèle would tremble no more at the thought of seeing her end up on the streets.

Had the neighbours who had been at the wedding thought of it? Their smiles, their congratulations, their contentment, especially at the end of the feast, were they sincere?

Weren't they, too, a little ashamed of the bargain which, in a sense, they had just countersigned?

The Abbé Grimault had not openly tried to dissuade him from his designs. Doubtless he, too, preferred to see Gina married. Nevertheless even Jonas's conversion had evoked little enthusiasm in him.

'I daren't ask you whether you have faith, since I would not wish to induce you to tell a lie.'

So he knew that Jonas didn't believe in it. Did he also guess that it had not been simply to marry Gina that he had become a Catholic and that he had sometimes thought about it long before he met her?

'I hope you will be happy with her, and bring her happiness.'

The good wish was genuine, but it could be seen that he placed little confidence in it. He did his duty as a priest in joining them together as he had done in receiving the little man from Archangel into the bosom of the Roman Catholic church.

How was it that during the two years it had never once occurred to Jonas that Gina could be afraid of him?

Now the scales had fallen from his eyes and details he had taken no notice of were coming back to him.

He was realizing, at last, that he was a foreigner, a Jew, a solitary, a man from the other end of the world who had come like a parasite to embed himself in the flesh of the Old Market.

'If you will come this way . . .'

The two men were ready with their hats on, and with Jonas between them, half a head smaller than either, they set off for the rue Haute in the hot, sun-soaked air.

'Did it go off all right?' asked Basquin, who had obviously been to have a word with his chief.

'I suppose so. I'm not sure.'

'The superintendent is a man of remarkable intelligence, who would have had an important post in Paris a long time ago if he didn't insist on living with his daughter. He was called to the bar at the age of twenty-three and started off his career with the prefecture. It was sheer accident that he joined the police.'

From time to time Basquin returned the greeting of a passer-by and people turned to stare at Jonas, who was walking between the two policemen.

'During the last four days, since the day I came to see you, we have been circulating your wife's description everywhere.'

The inspector was surprised at Jonas's lack of reaction and kept shooting him little glances out of the corner of his eye.

'True, there are plenty of pretty dark girls in red dresses. Quite apart from the fact that she may have bought herself a new dress.'

As he passed the restaurant, Jonas saw the top of Pepito's head above the curtains, and Pepito was looking at him. Would he be lunching there? Would they give him the chance? It was already half past eleven. They were probably going to search the house from top to bottom and the corners were full of odd bits and pieces, for Jonas never threw anything away.

Who could say, at this stage, that they were not going to arrest him?

It remained for him to pass Le Bouc's, and he decided to turn his head away, not from shame, but to spare them embarrassment.

For despite everything they must have been embarrassed. They must have egged one another on. Any one of them, on their own, with the exception of Frédo, would not have dared to turn against him so brutally.

'If you'll say it, then I'll say so too . . .'

Why not, since he had taken them in? He took the keys from his pocket and opened the door, under which he found a yellow cinema programme.

'Come in, gentlemen.'

The shop, which had had the sun all the morning and in which the air was stagnating, was like a furnace. Two great black flies were flying clumsily about.

'Presumably you would rather I left the door open?'

The smell of books was stronger than usual and, in order to create a draught, he went and opened the door into the yard, where a blackbird was hopping about. He knew it. The blackbird came every morning and was not afraid of Jonas.

'Call me if you need me.'

It was Basquin who took the lead.

'I'd like to visit the bedroom first. I suppose it's this way?'

'Go on up. I'll follow.'

He wanted a cup of coffee, but didn't dare ask for permission to go and make himself one, still less to go and have one at Le Bouc's.

The bedroom was tidy, the counterpane carefully spread on the bed, and the dressing-table immaculate. As he went in Jonas's eye fell immediately upon Gina's comb which was dirty, with one or two hairs caught in it. He was so used to seeing it in same place that he had not noticed it during the past few days, nor washed it.

'Is this the only bedroom in the house?'

'Yes.'

'So that this is the bed you both slept in?'

'Yes.'

Through the open window Jonas thought he could hear stealthy footsteps on the pavement, muffled whispers.

'Where does this door lead to?'

'The lavatory and bathroom.'

'And that one?'

He pushed it open. It had once been a bedroom looking out on to the yard, but it was so tiny that there was only just room for a bed. Jonas used it as a loft and box-room for his shop. It contained broken chairs, an old chest with the lock torn off, dating from their flight from Russia, a dressmaker's model, which he had bought for Gina and which she had never used, cracked crockery, piles of books, the ones which he had no hope of ever selling, and even a chamber pot. No one ever dusted this room. The skylight was not opened more than once a year and the air was musty, everything was covered with a layer of grey powder.

The two policemen exchanged glances. Presumably it meant that nobody could have gone in there recently without leaving traces. They had kept their hats on and Basquin was finishing a cigarette, the stub of which he went and threw down the lavatory.

'Are these the clothes?' he asked, pointing to the wardrobe with the looking-glass.

Jonas opened its two doors and the inspector ran his hand over the dresses, the coats, then over Jonas's two suits and overcoat.

'She didn't have another coat?'

'No.'

In the bottom of the wardrobe stood three pairs of Gina's shoes, a pair of slippers and a pair of his own shoes. That was their entire wardrobe.

'Is that the famous strong-box?'

He was thus admitting that the superintendent had spoken to him while Jonas was waiting in the front office.

'Do you mind opening it?'

He took out his keys again, put the strong-box on to the bed and raised the lid.

'I thought it was empty!' exclaimed Basquin.

'I never said that.'

There were in fact still about fifty transparent packets each containing a stamp or a stamped card.

'Well, what did she take?'

'About a quarter of the stamps which were in here. The whole lot, with the packets, wouldn't have fitted into her bag.'

'The rarest ones?'

'Yes.'

'How could she have recognized them?'

'I had shown them to her. And also because they were on top of the others, as I had just been looking at them.'

The two men exchanged glances behind his back, and they must have been thinking he was a lunatic.

'You don't have any weapons in the house?'

'No.'

'You have never possessed a revolver?'

'Never.'

The detective with Basquin was examining the floor, the woven carpet of blue and red flowers, the blue curtains, as if in search of traces of blood. He made an even more careful study around the dressing-table and went off to pursue his investigations in the bathroom.

Basquin stepped on to the straw-bottomed chair to look on top of the wardrobe, then he pulled open the drawers of the chest one by one.

The top one was Gina's drawer, and everything was in chaos, her three nightdresses, petticoats, brassières, combinations which she scarcely ever wore, stockings, an old bag, a powder case, two boxes of aspirin, and a small rubber object.

In the bag the inspector found a handkerchief stained with

lipstick, some coins, a propelling-pencil, and a receipt for 227 francs for a purchase she had made at Prisunic.

Jonas's drawer was in better order, with the shirts on one side, the pyjamas on the other, the socks, underpants, handkerchiefs, and vests in the middle. There was also a brand new wallet which Gina had given him for his birthday and he never used because he considered it too smart. It still smelled of new leather and was empty.

Lastly, the bottom drawer contained, thrown in anyhow, everything that had not found a home elsewhere, medicines, the two winter blankets, a silver-mounted hat brush given to them as a wedding present, some hairpins, and two advertisement ashtrays which they didn't use.

Basquin did not forget the drawer of the bedside table, where he found a pair of broken glasses, some gardenal, a razor, and finally a photograph of Gina naked.

It was not Jonas who had taken it, nor he who had put it there. It dated back to well before their marriage, for Gina could not have been more than twenty at the time and, if her bosom was already well-developed, her waist was narrower, her hips less powerful.

'Look,' she had said to him one day when, by a miracle, she was tidying up her things. 'Do you recognize me?'

The features were not very clearly defined. True, the photograph was blurred. Gina was standing at the foot of a bed, in a hotel bedroom probably, and it was obvious that she did not know what to do with her hands.

'Don't you think I was better looking than I am now?'

He had said no.

'It amuses me to keep it, because I can compare myself. The day will come when people will no longer believe it's me.'

She looked at herself in the glass, displaying her bosom, feeling her hips.

'I didn't take that photograph,' he told Basquin hurriedly. 'She was much younger then.'

The inspector glanced at it again, curiously.

'So I see,' he said.

Then, after a glance at his colleague:

'Let's take a look at the ground floor.'

It was rather like a public sale, when the most personal furniture and objects of a family are piled up in the street for inquisitive passers-by to come and finger them.

What did it matter now that they should turn his home inside out, after what had already been done to him?

Not only was he no longer at home in his own house, but he was no longer at home in his own skin.

Chapter Eight

As they passed through the little room on their way from the bedroom to the kitchen, Jonas glanced automatically in the direction of the shop and saw some faces pressed to the window; he even caught a glimpse of one urchin who must have ventured into the house, hurriedly beating a retreat and causing a burst of laughter.

The detectives examined everything, the cupboard where the groceries, the scales and the coffee-grinder were kept, the brooms hanging from its doors, the contents of the other cupboards, the table drawer, and they studied with particular attention the meat axe and the carving knives as if in search of tell-tale signs.

They went into the yard as well, where Basquin pointed to the windows of the Palestris' house.

'Isn't that Gina's home?'

'Yes.'

One of the windows actually belonged to the bedroom, now Frédo's, which she occupied as a young girl.

The little room took longer. The drawers were full of papers of all sorts, envelopes crammed with stamps, marked with signs which the inspector had to have explained, and for a long time he turned over the pages of the Russian album, with a series of sidelong glances at Jonas.

'You haven't done the same for the other countries, have you?'

He could only reply that he hadn't. He knew what they would deduce from that.

'I see you have the entire Soviet series. It's the first time I've had a chance of seeing them. How did you get hold of them?'

'You can pick them up everywhere in the trade.'

'Ah!'

The inquisitive eavesdroppers did not disappear until the two men set to work on the shop, where they ran their hands behind the rows of books.

'Have you dusted here recently?'

Was it also going to count against him that in order to keep himself occupied, he had undertaken a spring-cleaning of the shelves? It was all the same to him. He was no longer trying to defend himself.

At a particular moment during the morning, he could not have said precisely which moment, and in any case it did not matter, something had snapped. It was as if someone had cut a wire, or better still, perhaps, as if he had suddenly become independent of the law of gravity.

He could see the two of them, the inspector and Dambois, who were carrying out their duty conscientiously, but their comings and goings, their actions, the words they spoke, no longer had any connection with himself. A little knot of people outside continued to watch the house, and he did not even glance up to see whom it was composed of; for him they were nothing more than a patch of life in the sunlight.

He was beyond everything. He had passed to the other side. He was waiting, patiently, for his companions to finish, and when they finally made up their minds to depart, he removed the door handle and locked the door behind them. It was no longer his own house. Furniture and objects were still in the same place. He could still have placed his hand on each thing with his eyes closed, but all real contact had ceased to exist.

He was hungry. The idea of going to eat at Pepito's did not

occur to him. In the kitchen he found the remains of some cheese from the day before and a hunk of bread, and he began to eat, standing in front of the door into the backyard.

At that particular moment he had decided nothing, at least not consciously, and it was when his gaze alighted on a clothes line stretched between the house and the Chaignes' wall that his thoughts took a definite shape.

He had come by a long road, from Archangel to here, by way of Moscow, Yalta, and Constantinople to finish up in an old house in the Market Place. His father had gone back again. Then his mother.

'*I insist on this one at least remaining!*' Constantin Milk had said, pointing to Jonas at the moment of setting out on his adventure.

Now it was his turn. His decision was taken, but he still finished his cheese and bread with his eye first on the clothes line, which was made of twisted steel wire, then on the branch of the lime-tree which projected from the grocer's garden next door. One of the two iron chairs stood, by chance, directly beneath the branch.

It was true, as he had told the inspector, that he had never possessed a weapon and had a horror of all violence, so much so that the noise of children's pistols in the Square made him jump each time he heard it.

He was reflecting, wondering whether he had anything still to do upstairs, or in the shop or the little room.

He had nothing left to do anywhere. They hadn't understood him, or else he hadn't understood the others, and this latest misunderstanding was now beyond all hope of being cleared up.

He had a momentary impulse to explain everything in a letter, but it was a last vanity of which he was ashamed, and he rejected the idea.

He had some difficulty in undoing the knots by which the

metal cord was attached and he had to fetch the pliers from the kitchen drawer. He was not sad, or bitter. He felt, on the contrary, a serenity which he had never known before.

He was thinking of Gina, and now it was no longer Gina as other people saw her and as she saw herself, it was a disembodied Gina, confused in his mind with the image he had created of his sister Doussia, a woman such as probably does not exist: Woman.

Would she find out that he had died because of her? He was trying to lie to himself again, and it made him blush. It was not on her account that he was departing, it was on his own account, perhaps in fact it was because he had been forced, in his own eyes, to stoop too far.

Could he go on living after what he had discovered about himself and about the others?

He climbed on to the iron chair to attach the cord to the branch of the tree and grazed his finger-tip on a loose strand of wire; it bled, and he sucked it, as he used to do when he was a little boy.

Although you could see the kitchen door from the Palestris' window, from the bedroom that used to be Gina's, the Chaignes' party wall blocked the view from where he was standing. All he had to do now was to make a slip knot and he used the pliers so as to be sure that it would hold.

A hot nausea suddenly rose to his head at the sight of the loop which hung suspended, and he wiped his brow and upper lip, had difficulty in swallowing his saliva.

He felt ridiculous standing on the iron chair, hesitating, trembling, seized with panic at the thought of the physical pain which he was going to feel, and worse still, of the slow choking, of the struggle which his body, hanging in mid-air, would instinctively make against suffocation.

What was preventing him from living, after all? The sun would continue to shine, the rain to fall, the Square to be filled with the sounds and smells of market day. He was still capable of making himself coffee, alone in the kitchen, listening to the songs of the birds.

The blackbird, just then, his blackbird, came and perched on the box where the chives were growing, beside a tuft of thyme, and as he watched it hopping about, Jonas's eyes filled with tears.

There was no need for him to die. Nobody was forcing him. With patience and an extra effort of humility, he could still come to terms with himself.

He stepped down from the iron chair and suddenly ran into the house in order to flee from the temptation, to be sure of not turning back. He struck a match over the gas ring, poured some water into the kettle to make himself some coffee.

He would find good reasons for acting as he was. Who could tell? Perhaps Gina would come back one day and would need him. Even the people from the market would understand, in the end. Hadn't Fernand Le Bouc already shown signs of embarrassment?

In the semi-darkness of the cupboard, he ground the coffee-mill, which was fixed to the wall. It was a china mill, with a Dutch landscape in a blue on a white background, and a picture of a windmill. He had never been to Holland. He, who as a baby had covered such immense distances, had never travelled since, as though he had been afraid of losing his place in the Old Market.

He would be patient. The superintendent, Basquin had told him, was an intelligent man.

Already the smell of coffee was doing him good, while the steam misted over his glasses. He mused to himself, whether he would have kept his glasses on to hang himself, then he thought of Doussia again, telling himself that perhaps it was thanks to her that he had not taken the final step.

He did not yet dare to return to the yard to undo the knot.

The alarm clock, on the mantelpiece, pointed to ten to two and it comforted him to hear its familiar tick.

He would come to terms with himself, avoid thinking about certain subjects. He felt an urge to see his Russian stamps again, as though to cling on to something, and, taking his cup with him, he went and sat at his desk in the little room.

Was he a coward? Would he regret not having done today what he had decided to do? If life became too burdensome later on, would he still have the courage to do it?

There was nobody in sight outside. The Square was empty. The clock of St Cecilia's struck two and according to the rites, he ought to have replaced the handle in the door.

It no longer had the same importance as it had before, and he had plenty of time to return to his old habits bit by bit. He opened the drawer and took out the album, on the first page of which he had gummed a photograph of his father and mother outside their fishmongery. He had taken it with a cheap camera which he had been given for Christmas at the age of eleven. He was just going to turn over the page when a shadow outlined itself against the shop-window. A woman he did not know was knocking at the door, trying to see inside, surprised to find the shop shut.

He thought it was a customer and almost did not open the door. It was a working-class woman about forty years old, and she must have borne several children and worked hard all her life for one could see in her the deformities, the lassitude of women of that type, grown old before their time.

Shielding her eyes with her hand, she was peering into the obscurity of the shop, and in the end he rose to his feet, almost out of charity.

'I was afraid there was nobody at home,' she said, looking at him curiously.

He said quietly:

'I was working.'

'You are Gina's husband?'

'Yes.'

'Is it true they mean to arrest you?'

'I don't know.'

'They told me so this morning, and I wondered if I would be too late.'

'Won't you sit down?' he said, pointing to a chair.

'I haven't time. I must get back to the hotel. They don't know I've come out yet, as I took the back door. The management's new in the business and seem to think they've got to be strict.'

He listened without understanding.

'I work as a chambermaid at the Commercial Hotel. Do you know it?'

It was there that he had attended the wedding reception of Ancel's daughter. The walls were painted in imitation marble and the hall was bedecked with green plants.

'Before my husband went to the factory I used to live in this area, at the corner of the rue Gambetta and the rue des Saules. I knew Gina well when she must have been about fifteen years old. That's why I recognized her at once when she came to the hotel.'

'When has she been to the hotel?'

'Several times. Each time the traveller from Paris comes here, that's to say nearly every two weeks. It's been going on for months now. He's called Thierry, Jacques Thierry. I looked up his name in the register, and he's in chemical products. Seems he's an engineer, though he's still young. I'd bet he's not yet thirty. He's married and has two lovely children. I know because to start with he always put a photo of his family on the bedside table. His wife's a blonde. His eldest, a boy, is five or six, like my youngest.

'I don't know where he met Gina but one afternoon I saw him in the corridor with her and she went into his bedroom.

'Since then, every time he's come, she stops in to see him at the hotel for an hour or two, all according, and I'm the last one to be in the dark about what goes on, since it's me that has to remake the bed. Begging your pardon for telling you, but they say you've been in trouble and I thought it might be better for you to know.

'Gina was like that at fifteen, if that's any consolation, and I should add something that you perhaps don't know but I'm told by people who ought to know, and that is that her mother was the same before her.'

'Did she go to the hotel on Wednesday last week?'

'Yes. Around half past two. When they told me the story, this morning, I wasn't sure of the day and went and looked at the register. He arrived early on Tuesday and left again on Wednesday evening.'

'By train?'

'No. He always comes by car. I gather he has other factories to visit on his way.'

'Were they together a long time, on Wednesday?'

'Same as usual,' she replied, with a shrug.

'What dress was she wearing?'

'A red dress. You couldn't help noticing.'

He wanted to be sure.

'Now I would rather not get mixed in the affair because as I told you before, the management's got its own ideas. But if they really mean to put you in prison and there isn't any other way, I will repeat what I've told you.'

'You haven't got the address of this man in Paris?'

'I copied it down on a piece of paper and brought it with me.'

She seemed surprised to see him so unmoved and so gloomy, when she must have expected him to feel relieved.

'It's number 27 rue Championnet. I don't suppose he'll have taken her home. When I think of his wife, who looks so delicate, and his children . . .'

'I am most grateful to you.'

'My name is Berthe Lenoir, in case you need me. I would rather no one came to the hotel. We live in the housing estate opposite the factory, the second block on the right, the one with blue shutters.'

He thanked her again and, when he was left alone, felt more disconcerted than ever, rather like a prisoner who, recovering his freedom after many long years, does not know what to do with it.

He could furnish them with proof now that he had not disposed of Gina and that he had not thrown her body into the canal. What surprised him most was what he had been told about the man she had gone off with, for he did not correspond to the type she usually chose.

Their affair had been going on for about six months and during the whole of that time she had not run away once.

Was she in love with him? And he, was he going to break up his household? Given her situation, why had Gina taken the stamps?

Mechanically he had put on his hat and was heading for the door, in order to go to the police station. This seemed to him to be the only logical thing to do. It could do no harm to Gina who, the moment the complaint was withdrawn, had nothing to answer the police for. He would not claim back his stamps. They had nothing against her lover either.

It was a curious sensation to find himself on the pavement once more, in the sun, which was even hotter than in the morning, and to pass Le Bouc's, telling himself that he would be going back there again.

For there was nothing to stop him going back. The people of the market would soon find out what had happened and, instead of holding it against him, would be sorry for him. They would be a bit ashamed at first, for having deserted him so quickly, but it only needed a few days for everything to be

once again as it had been in the past, and for them to call out
cheerfully:

'Good morning, Monsieur Jonas!'

Would Angèle be cross with him for not having kept a better
watch on her daughter? Had she been able to do so herself,
before Gina's marriage?

Only Frédo would not change his attitude, but there was a
very small chance of Frédo becoming reconciled with the
human race. He would sooner or later go off, God knows where,
far away from the Vieux-Marché which he hated, and would
be just as unhappy somewhere else.

He very nearly went into Fernand's there and then, as if it
were all forgotten already, then he told himself that it was too
soon, and set off up the rue Haute.

He was convinced that Gina would come back, as she had
always done before, only more marked this time, and that then
she would need him.

Hadn't everything become easy? He would go into the police
station, walk over to the black wooden counter dividing the
first room in two.

'I want to speak to Superintendent Devaux, please.'

'What name?'

Unless it was the same sergeant as that morning, who would
be sure to recognize him.

'Jonas Milk.'

For here they called him Milk. It hardly mattered, this time,
if they kept him waiting. The superintendent would be
surprised. His first thought would be that he had resolved to
make a clean breast of everything.

'I know where my wife is,' Jonas would announce.

He would provide him with the name and address of the
chambermaid and advise him not to go and see her at the hotel;
he would also hand over the piece of paper with the address of
the traveller in chemical goods.

'You can check up, but I must insist on their not being troubled. Madame Thierry may very well know nothing, but there's no point in telling her the truth.'

Would they understand him this time? Were they going to look on him again as a man from another planet? Or would they at last condescend to consider him as a human being, like other human beings?

The rue Haute, at that hour, was almost deserted. In the Place de l'Hôtel de Ville the costermongers' carts had disappeared and a few pigeons were still foraging among the cobblestones.

He saw the bird-cages in the distance, opposite the police station, but he could not hear the cock crowing.

That morning in the superintendent's office he had fainted for the first time in his life and it had not been an unpleasant sensation; it had even seemed to him at one moment that his body no longer weighed anything, as if he were in the process of becoming disembodied. At the moment of losing consciousness he had thought of Doussia.

He was slowing his pace without realizing. He had only another twenty yards to cover and he could see distinctly the round eyes of the parrot on its perch. A policeman came out of the station and mounted a bicycle, possibly on his way to deliver a summons on coarse paper like the one he had received the day before.

Was it really the day before? It seemed such a long way off! Hadn't he lived since then, almost as much as during the rest of his existence?

He had stopped ten paces from the door with the blue lantern above it and, with his eyes wide open, stood staring at nothing. A boy of about fifteen who was running by collided with him, almost knocked him down, and he just caught hold of his glasses in time. What would have happened if they had broken on the pavement?

The bird-seller, wearing a dark grey smock like an iron-monger's, was watching him, wondering perhaps if he had been taken ill, and Jonas turned about, once again crossed the Square with the small cobblestones and went down the rue Haute.

Pepito, who was sweeping out his restaurant with his door open, saw him pass. So did Le Bouc. There was only a little girl with very fair hair, who was playing dolls all by herself beneath the slate roofs of the Old Market, to watch him as he removed the handle from his door.

Chapter Nine

It was a dull grey day. A small lorry was parking, two of its wheels on the pavement, opposite the bookseller's shop. The baker's wife hadn't noticed that he had not appeared that morning to buy his three croissants. The boy who had taken a book on bees the week before and was bringing in his fifty francs, tried to open the door and looked inside without seeing anything.

At a quarter past ten, in Le Bouc's, Ancel remarked:

'Odd! Jonas hasn't been in this morning.'

He added, but without malice:

'Little bastard!'

Le Bouc had said nothing.

It was only at eleven o'clock that, in Angèle's shop, a woman who had tried to go in the shop to buy a book had asked:

'Is your son-in-law ill?'

Angèle had retorted, leaning over a basket of spinach, with her great behind in the air:

'If he is, I hope he croaks!'

Which had not prevented her from asking:

'Why do you say that?'

'His shop's shut.'

'Can they have arrested him already?'

A little while later, when she was free of customers, she went to have a look for herself, pressed her face to the window, but everything appeared to be in order within the house except for Jonas's hat, which stood on a straw-bottomed chair.

'Have you seen Jonas, Mélanie?' she asked, on her way past the Chaignes.

'Not this morning.'

When Louis came back, and parked his three-wheeler, she told him:

'It seems Jonas has been arrested.'

'So much the better.'

'The handle isn't in the door and I couldn't see anything going on inside.'

Louis went for a drink at Le Bouc's.

'They've arrested Jonas.'

Constable Benaiche was there, having a glass of white wine.

'Who?'

'The police, I presume.'

Benaiche frowned, shrugged his shoulders, and said:

'Strange.'

Then he emptied his glass.

'I didn't hear anything up at the station.'

The only one to seem uneasy was Le Bouc. He said nothing, but, after a few minutes' thought, he retired to the back room where there was a telephone on the wall by the lavatory door.

'Get me the police station, please.'

'The number's ringing now.'

'Police here.'

He recognized the sergeant's voice.

'That you, Jouve?'

'Who's that?'

'Le Bouc. I say, is it true that you've arrested Jonas?'

'The bookseller?'

'Yes.'

'I haven't heard anything about him this morning. But it doesn't concern me. Wait a second.'

His voice came back, a little while later:

'No one here knows anything about it. The superintendent's out to lunch, but Basquin, who's here, would have heard.'

'His door's closed.'

'So what?'

'I don't know. No one's seen him this morning.'

'I'd better put you on to the inspector. Hang on.'

Another pause, and it was Basquin's voice:

'Jouve tells me Jonas hasn't been seen today?'

'Yes. His shop's shut. There's nothing going on inside.'

'Do you think he would have gone?'

That was not what Fernand had in mind, but he preferred not to volunteer any opinion.

'I don't know. It seems odd to me. He's a queer chap.'

'I'll be right round.'

When he arrived ten minutes later, several people emerged from the bar and walked over to Jonas's shop.

The inspector knocked at the door, normally at first, then louder and louder, finally called out, looking up towards the open window on the first floor.

Angèle, who had come up, had lost her habitual caustic wit.

'Monsieur Jonas!'

At Fernand's, Louis, who was gulping down two glasses of *grappa* one after the other, growled:

'I'll bet he's gone to earth in some corner, like a rat.'

He didn't believe it. He was blustering, uneasiness reflected in his red-rimmed eyes.

'Is there a locksmith nearby?' asked Basquin, who had tried shaking the door in vain.

'Old Deltour. He lives in . . .'

Madame Chaigne interrupted the woman who was speaking.

'It's not worth the trouble of forcing the door. You only have to get over the wall of the yard by climbing on a chair. Follow me, inspector.'

She led him through her shop, then through the kitchen

where a stew was simmering, as far as the yard, which was littered with barrels and crates.

'It's Jonas!' she called out as she passed her husband, who was hard of hearing.

Then:

'Look! A barrel will do even better than a chair.'

She remained standing, in her white apron, her hands on her hips, watching the inspector hoisting himself on to the wall.

'Can you get down the other side?'

He did not reply at once, for he had just found the little man from Archangel hanging from the branch which grew out over the yard. The kitchen door was open with, on the wax table-cloth, a cup containing the remains of some coffee, and a blackbird crossed the doorstep, coming from inside the house, and flew off to the top of the lime tree where it had its nest.

The Simenon Novels

1931

Le relais d'Alsace (The Man from Everywhere)

1932

Le passager du 'Polarlys' (The Mystery of the 'Polarlys')

1933

Les fiançailles de M. Hire (Mr Hire's Engagement)
Le coup de lune (Tropic Moon)
La maison du canal (The House by the Canal)
L'Ane-Rouge (The Night Club)
Les gens d'en face (The Window over the Way)
Le haut mal (The Woman of the Grey House)
L'homme de Londres (Newhaven–Dieppe)

1934

Le locataire (The Lodger)
Les suicidés (One Way Out)

1935

Les Pitard (*A Wife at Sea*)
Les clients d'Avrenos
Quartier nègre

1936

L'évadé (*The Disintegration of J.P.G.*)
Long cours (*The Long Exile*)
Les demoiselles de Concarneau (*The Breton Sisters*)
45° à l'ombre (*Aboard the Aquitaine*)

1937

Le testament Donadieu (*The Shadow Falls*)
L'assassin (*The Murderer*)
Le blanc à lunettes (*Talatala*)
Faubourg (*Home Town*)

1938

Ceux de la soif
Chemin sans issue (*Blind Path*)
Les rescapés du Télémaque (*The Survivors*)
Les trois crimes de mes amis
Le suspect (*The Green Thermos*)
Les soeurs Lacroix (*Poisoned Relations*)
Touriste de bananes (*Banana Tourist*)
M. La Souris (*Monsieur La Souris*)
La Marie du Port (*Chit of a Girl*)
L'homme qui regardait passer les trains (*The Man Who
   Watched the Trains Go by*)
Le cheval blanc (*The White Horse Inn*)

1939

Le coup de vague
Chez Krull (*Chez Krull*)
Le bourgmestre de Furnes (*The Burgomaster of Furnes*)

1940

Malempin (*The Family Lie*)
Les inconnus dans la maison (*The Strangers in the House*)

1941

Cour d'assises (*Justice*)
Bergelon (*The Country Doctor*)
L'outlaw (*The Outlaw*)
Il pleut, bergère . . . (*Black Rain*)
Le voyageur de la Toussaint (*Strange Inheritance*)
La maison de sept jeunes filles

1942

Oncle Charles s'est enfermé
La veuve Couderc (*Ticket of Leave*)
Le fils Cardinaud (*Young Cardinaud*)
La vérité sur Bébé Donge (*The Trial of Bébé Donge*)

1944

Le rapport du gendarme (*The Gendarme's Report*)

1945

La fuite de M. Monde (*Monsieur Monde Vanishes*)
La fenêtre des Rouet (*Across the Street*)
L'aîné des Ferchaux (*The First-born*)

1946

Les noces de Poitiers (*The Couple from Poitiers*)
Le cercle de Mahé

1947

Trois chambres à Manhattan (*Three Beds in Manhattan*)
Au bout du rouleau
Lettre à mon juge (*Act of Passion*)
Le destin des Malou (*The Fate of the Malous*)
Le clan des Ostendais (*The Ostenders*)
Le passager clandestin (*The Stowaway*)

1948

Le bilan Malétras (*The Reckoning*)
La jument perdue
La neige était sale (*The Stain on the Snow*)
Pedigree (*Pedigree*)

1949

Le fond de la bouteille (*The Bottom of the Bottle*)
Les fantômes du chapelier (*The Hatter's Ghosts*)
Les quatre jours du pauvre homme (*Four Days in a Lifetime*)

1950

Un nouveau dans la ville
L'enterrement de M. Bouvet (*The Burial of Monsieur Bouvet*)
Les volets verts (*The Heart of a Man*)

1951

Tante Jeanne (*Aunt Jeanne*)
Le temps d'Anaïs (*The Girl in his Past*)
Une vie comme neuve (*A New Lease of Life*)

1952

Marie qui louche (*The Girl with a Squint*)
La mort de Belle (*Belle*)
Les frères Rico (*The Brothers Rico*)

1953

Antoine et Julie (*The Magician*)
L'escalier de fer (*The Iron Staircase*)
Feux rouges (*Red Lights*)

1954

Crime impuni (*The Fugitive*)
L'horloger d'Everton (*The Watchmaker of Everton*)
Le grand Bob (*Big Bob*)

1955

Les témoins (The Witnesses)
La boule noire

1956

Les complices (The Accomplices)
En cas de malheur (In Case of Emergency)
Le petit homme d'Arkhangelsk (The Little Man from
   Archangel)

1957

Le fils (The Son)
Le nègre (The Negro)

1958

Strip-tease (Striptease)
Le président (The Premier)
Le passage de la ligne
Dimanche (Sunday)

1959

La vieille (The Grandmother)
Le veuf (The Widower)

1960

L'ours en peluche (Teddy Bear)

1961

Betty (Betty)
Le train (The Train)

1962

La porte (The Door)
Les autres (The Others)

1963

Les anneaux de Bicêtre (The Patient)

1964

La chambre bleue (The Blue Room)
L'homme au petit chien (The Man with the Little Dog)

1965

Le petit saint (The Little Saint)
Le train de Venise (The Venice Train)

1966

Le confessionnal (The Confessional)
La mort d'Auguste (The Old Man Dies)

1967

Le chat (The Cat)
Le déménagement (The Neighbours)

1968

La prison (The Prison)
La main (The Man on the Bench in the Barn)

1969

Il y a encore des noisetiers
Novembre (November)

1970

Le riche homme (The Rich Man)

1971

La disparition d'Odile (The Disappearance of Odile)
La cage de verre (The Glass Cage)

1972

Les innocents (The Innocents)